"Get the Field Dress unit to fix you up with a wardrobe. You'd better take several gowns, a couple of cocktail dresses and bikinis. You'll only need the bottoms, of course."

"Of course." Mackenzie tried not to bat an eye. She knew that everyone went topless on European beaches except prudish, self-conscious American tourists. No way she wanted Nick to know she'd fallen smack into the prude category.

"What about my cover?"

Nick made a show of pulling down his cuffs, and Mackenzie knew what was coming. The man had a tabloid reputation to live up to, after all.

"The best cover is always the simplest. When asked, we'll merely introduce ~~you as~~ my compan~~ion.~~"

"Define ~~...~~"

"Friend. ~~...~~"

"I don't ~~...~~ ~~...~~ed. "Let's go with busi~~ness~~ associate."

Amusement flickered in Nick's eyes. "Do you really think the French will make any distinction between the two?"

"The French might not, but we will."

Dear Reader,

Welcome to another month of the most exciting romantic reading around, courtesy of Silhouette Intimate Moments. Starting things off with a bang, we have *To Love a Thief* by ultrapopular Merline Lovelace. This newest CODE NAME: DANGER title takes you back into the supersecret world of the Omega Agency for a dangerous liaison you won't soon forget.

For military romance, Catherine Mann's WINGMEN WARRIORS are the ones to turn to. These uniformed heroes and heroines are irresistible, and once you join Darcy Renshaw and Max Keagan for a few *Private Maneuvers,* you won't even be trying to resist, anyway. Wendy Rosnau continues her unflashed miniseries THE BROTHERHOOD in *Last Man Standing,* while Sharon Mignerey's couple find themselves *In Too Deep.* Finally, welcome two authors who are new to the line but not to readers. Kristen Robinette makes an unforgettable entrance with *In the Arms of a Stranger,* and Ana Leigh offers a matchup between *The Law and Lady Justice.*

I hope you enjoy all six of these terrific novels, and that you'll come back next month for more of the most electrifying romantic reading around.

Enjoy!

Leslie Wainger

Leslie J. Wainger
Executive Editor

Please address questions and book requests to:
Silhouette Reader Service
U.S.: 3010 Walden Ave., P.O. Box 1325, Buffalo, NY 14269
Canadian: P.O. Box 609, Fort Erie, Ont. L2A 5X3

MERLINE LOVELACE

To Love a Thief

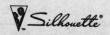

INTIMATE MOMENTS™

Published by Silhouette Books

America's Publisher of Contemporary Romance

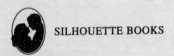 SILHOUETTE BOOKS

ISBN 0-373-27295-2

TO LOVE A THIEF

This edition published by arrangement with Harlequin Books S.A.

® and TM are trademarks of Harlequin Books S.A., used under license.
Trademarks indicated with ® are registered in the United States Patent
and Trademark Office, the Canadian Trade Marks Office and in other
countries.

Visit us at www.eHarlequin.com

Printed in U.S.A.

MERLINE LOVELACE

spent twenty-three years in the U.S. Air Force, pulling
tours in Vietnam, at the Pentagon and all over the world.
When she hung up her uniform, she decided to try her
hand at writing. Since then she's had more than forty novels published, with over six million copies of her work in
print. She and her own handsome hero live in Oklahoma.
They enjoy traveling and chasing little white balls around
the fairways.

Look for Merline in the Silhouette anthology *In Love and
War*, coming in August 2003.

Prologue

Yanking open the passenger door of a nondescript gray sedan, a heavyset male dropped into the seat. He brought with him just enough of the crisp September breeze to stir the stale odors of old French fries and half-eaten donuts that permeated the vehicle.

His nose wrinkled in disgust. "I wish to hell you'd dump your garbage in a trash can instead of tossing it in the back seat."

"Never mind my garbage," the driver growled. "Did you get through?"

"I got through."

"What was the message that was so damn important we had to call today?"

"Our client's getting antsy. Real antsy."

The driver crumpled his foam coffee cup and tossed it over his shoulder to join the rest of the litter. Scowling, he glared at his associate.

"Hell! This isn't like taking down a two-bit pusher or some husband who can't keep his pants zipped. We've been trying to set up the job for a week now. The target never takes the same route to work, never eats at the same restaurant two nights in a row and has a security system tougher to crack than Fort Knox, for God's sake!"

"So tell me something I don't know."

The retort earned him a hard, swift look. More than a little afraid of the man beside him, the passenger gulped and delivered the rest of the message that had come through the phone via a voice synthesizer that completely disguised the speaker's age, sex and nationality.

"We gotta do it within twenty-four hours or the deal's off."

His mouth set, the driver hunched his arms over the wheel. He'd been in the business long enough to know his reputation was on the line here. He'd accepted the contract, demanded and received a five-figure advance. If he didn't deliver as promised, he could kiss off the rest of the hefty fee he'd been promised. Worse, word would soon get around. Before long, he'd be back to shooting out the kneecaps of gamblers who welched on their debts at a hundred bucks a pop.

"All right," he snarled. "We'll do it tonight."

Chapter 1

From the outside, the elegant, three-story Federal-style town house looked much like its neighbors. It sat midblock on a quiet, tree-shaded street just off Massachusetts Avenue, in the heart of Washington's embassy district. The last rays of the afternoon sun glinted on its tall windows. Ivy meandered over its mellow red brick and almost obscured the discreet bronze plaque beside the front door.

The plaque identified the town house as home to the Offices of the President's Special Envoy. Savvy politicians and diplomats knew the position was created years ago to reward a wealthy campaign contributor with a yen for a fancy title and a hankering to rub elbows with the powerful elite. Like so many other fabricated posts in the nation's capital, the position had since taken on a staff and a life of its own.

Only a handful of insiders knew the special envoy also served as director of an agency whose initials comprised the last letter of the Greek alphabet: an agency so secret that its director reported only to the president. So supercharged that OMEGA's agents were activated only as a last resort, when other government agencies like the military, the FBI or the CIA couldn't respond for political or legal reasons.

For almost a year now, Nick Jensen had served as acting director of OMEGA. The wealth and international contacts he'd accumulated as owner of a string of outrageously high-priced watering holes for the rich and famous—not to mention his hefty contributions to the president's reelection campaign—had given him the necessary cachet for the special envoy's title.

But it was Nick's years as one of OMEGA's field agents that had given him the expertise to run the supersecret organization. He hadn't sought or particularly wanted the responsibility of sending his fellow operatives into harm's way, but Maggie Sinclair, the previous director, had convinced the president that Nick was the best person for the job.

Few people could hold out against Maggie when she set her mind to something. Nick was no exception—as the present situation indicated.

"You can't fail me, Lightning! I'm desperate."

Her voice floated over the speakers in the third-floor control center where Mackenzie Blair, OMEGA's chief of communications, had patched her straight through to the director.

"The woman stormed out the moment I walked into the house," Maggie exclaimed in exasperation. "Didn't give notice. Didn't offer an explanation. Just grabbed her purse and rushed right past me."

"Let me guess." Tapping his twenty-four karat gold Mont Blanc pen against the console in front of him, Nick had no difficulty picturing the scene. "She had grape jelly in her hair, muddy paw prints all down her front and lizard spit decorating her blouse."

A gurgle of laughter came over the speakers. "Actually, the grape jelly was on her shoes and the lizard spit was dribbling down her right cheek."

Chuckling, Nick leaned back in his chair. "How many nannies have you and Adam run through in the past six months? Two? Three?"

He caught the eyes of the dark-haired woman on the other side of the console. Grinning, Mackenzie held up four fingers.

"The body count doesn't matter," Maggie answered loftily. "What matters is that I don't have a baby-sitter available for tonight. I can't miss this banquet, Nick. Adam's worked too hard and too long. He deserves this recognition for his work with the International Monetary Fund. I may be eight months pregnant, but I'm going to pour myself into an evening gown and strap on high heels. If I can take those extreme measures, you ought to be willing to hold down the fort for a few hours. Can you be here by seven?"

Nick gave the computerized status board on the far wall a quick glance. He had one agent in Saudi Arabia. Another agent was on his way back to D.C. after weeks in Honduras and would need to be debriefed sometime tonight. Nick was also expected at a black-tie party thrown by one of Washington's most sophisticated hostesses.

But this was Maggie Sinclair. Code name Chameleon. A young, scrawny Nick had once offered to act as her pimp. It didn't even occur to him to refuse her this small service. Although he had to admit, the thought of spending several hours with the nonadult residents of her chaotic household daunted even OMEGA's acting director. Once again his glance drifted to the woman on the other side of the console.

"I'll be there by seven," he promised, his blue eyes on his chief of communications. "But I'm not going in alone, unarmed and without backup. I'll bring Mackenzie with me. We can get some work done after the girls are in bed.''

The grin fell off his chief of communications's face. With a little squawk, she bolted upright in her chair and waved both hands in a frantic negative. Maggie must have caught the strangled sound. Hastily, she terminated the conversation before either Nick or Mackenzie could weasel out.

''Great! See you both then.''

The thump of her receiver dropping down echoed through the speakers. The communications techs manning their posts turned away to hide their grins as their chief shoved out of her chair, planted both palms on the console, and directed an evil glare at her boss.

''Thanks a lot! I'm still flaking green dandruff from the last time I baby-sat for Maggie and Adam. Jilly swore that spray-on hair paint would wash out with a good shampoo.''

''Serves you right for not reading the directions on the can first.''

''Jilly *said* they'd tested it on Radizwell.''

''Well, that explains the dog's new shaved-to-the-skin look,'' Nick drawled. ''Normally his coat is so thick Adam has to use pruning shears to cut it.''

Realizing he was less than sympathetic to either

her or the sheepdog's misadventures with Jilly's paint can, Mackenzie changed tactics.

"You might consult me before volunteering my services as a baby-sitter," she huffed. "I could have plans for tonight."

"Do you?"

He knew the answer before she pursed her lips and shot him another nasty look.

Everyone at OMEGA agreed their chief of communications was a wizard at all things electronic. Since taking over the job, she'd provided field agents with miniaturized devices powerful enough to drop do-wrongs with a single zap, capture the smallest images in stunning digital detail from miles away and detect sounds as soft as a sneaker tread two floors down.

Everyone at OMEGA also agreed Mackenzie Blair needed to get a life. A short, disastrous marriage to another navy officer had spurred her decision to opt out of the military. It had also left her distinctly wary of entanglements. Since joining the OMEGA team, she'd spent most of her waking hours on the job. From all indications, her social life was nonexistent. Nick knew for a fact her evening meals usually consisted of pizza or fast food scarfed down right here at the control center.

More and more of late, he'd found himself contemplating ways to add variety to her diet...and

spice up her social life. Particularly after a recent
mission in San Antonio, when Mackenzie had
stepped out of her role of chief of communications
and into the arms of an overmuscled building contractor who'd hired a hit man to murder his wife.
She'd snuggled up to the bastard, wearing a low-
cut dress that spiked the temperature of every male
within a fifty-yard radius. Nick's temperature had
shot off the charts, as well. So, it seemed, had his
objectivity where this green-eyed brunette was con-
cerned.

Not that she had any clue how much she'd come
to occupy his thoughts. Nick was her boss. For the
time being, anyway. His professional code of ethics
wouldn't allow him to hit on someone who worked
for him. Hers, he knew, had been shaped by her
years in the navy, where fraternization between the
ranks was strictly taboo.

But when Maggie had her baby and returned to
work, Nick thought with a sudden tightening in his
groin, he fully intended to make his move.

If Maggie ever came back to work, that is.

The prospects were looking dimmer and dimmer
with each passing month and additional project she
became involved with. As she'd informed Nick on
several occasions, he might just have to get used to
serving as OMEGA's director. Shoving that thought

aside, he offered the still reluctant Mackenzie a bribe.

"Why don't I fix us dinner at Maggie and Adam's place? I'll bring the ingredients. And the wine," he added, remembering an especially fine white he'd just added to his private cellar.

She hesitated for several moments. Nick read the doubt in her eyes. Like him, she'd sensed the subtle changes in their relationship over the past few months. Unlike him, she hadn't yet made up her mind what to do about it.

"Dinner sounds good," she conceded, but in the next breath made it clear she intended to keep matters strictly professional. "As you said, we can use the time to get some work done. I want to wait for Ace to check in before I leave, though. He's scheduled to transmit a status report at six forty-five, our time."

Nick nodded. He'd spoken with Ace yesterday and knew the agent had as yet turned up no leads as to the saboteurs responsible for the explosions that ripped through several oil refineries in Saudi Arabia. The outraged Saudis had put a million dollar bounty on the person or persons responsible for the bombings. So far, the reward hadn't produced any results. Nor, it appeared, had Ace, who was slogging it out undercover in the oil fields with his Saudi counterpart.

"Contact me immediately if the report doesn't come through."

At the whiplike command, OMEGA's chief of communications snapped to attention and popped a salute. "Aye-aye, Skipper!"

Nick's features relaxed into a grin. "As you were, Blair. See you at seven."

The man moved like a lion, Mackenzie decided as he strolled out of the control center. All supreme confidence, sleek muscle and lethal grace. He looked like one, too, damn him. Forget the cashmere sports coats. Never mind the silk ties and Italian leather shoes. With his dark gold hair and tanned skin, he would have been right at home roaming the African plains.

Well, Mackenzie had let one too-handsome beast maul both her heart and her pride. She wasn't about to let another get close enough to sink his teeth in.

She dropped back into her chair, her mouth twisting in wry acknowledgment. Okay, so maybe her pride had suffered more than her heart. Even before she returned early from a cruise and caught her ex in bed with their well-endowed neighbor, Mackenzie had accepted the bitter fact that their marriage was over. She would have chosen a more civilized way to end it, though.

The mere memory of the very hard, very swift

knee she'd planted in David's groin when he'd grabbed her arm and tried to force her to listen to his pathetic excuses was enough to produce a grin. Whistling cheerfully, she went back to work.

Later that evening, Mackenzie used the short drive to Maggie and Adam's house to prepare herself. She respected Adam, who'd served as OMEGA's director before Maggie, but her loyalty was to his wife, who'd hired her right out of the navy. Mackenzie considered Maggie her friend as well as her mentor. What's more, she thoroughly enjoyed the tales of Chameleon's outrageous exploits the other OMEGA agents frequently repeated and, she suspected, greatly exaggerated.

Friend or no friend, however, no one entered Maggie and Adam's elegant Georgetown residence without putting themselves in a mental brace. Controlled mayhem was the kindest way—the only way!—to describe their chaotic household.

Maggie's pet iguana was bad enough. The thing was the size of a small dog, had a foot-long tongue and devoured plants, newspaper and shoes indiscriminately. Making matters worse was a pony-size Hungarian sheepdog, a gift from the vice president who'd wanted desperately to get rid of the oversize, overfriendly beast.

Unfortunately, Radizwell had recently developed a bad case of the hots for the blue-and-orange, bug-eyed iguana. He was always trying to hump the hissing, spitting lizard. His enthusiastic efforts wreaked havoc on nearby furniture, had Adam gritting his teeth and made Maggie's small daughters shriek with laughter. Mackenzie didn't even want to *think* about the stories four-year-old Jilly shared with her friends and teachers at nursery school.

When she pulled into the circular drive leading to Adam and Maggie's two-story home, she saw Nick had already arrived. She pulled up behind his Jag, trying hard not to drool over its gleaming black beauty, and made for the front door. Adam Ridgeway, code name Thunder, answered the tinkling call of the chimes.

Mackenzie gulped. Nick Jensen in tan cashmere and navy slacks was enough to make any woman swallow her tongue. Adam Ridgeway in white tie and tails could make her forget she ever had one.

If Mackenzie hadn't sworn off men for the foreseeable future...

If this suave, aristocratic Bostonian wasn't married to her idol...

If he weren't carrying one dark-haired cherub in the crook of his right arm and had another tucked under his left...

"'Kenzie!''

The squeal came from the youngest, a bright-eyed two-year-old. Thrusting out her chubby arms, she demanded an instant embrace. With a smile for Adam, Mackenzie gathered Samantha into her arms. Her smile took a quick downward tilt when an ear-shattering woof boomed through the hall. Whirling, Adam rapped out a sharp command.

"No!"

Radizwell put out all four paws and tried to stop. He really tried. Claws clicking on the slick tiles, he slid a good three yards before careening past Adam, who managed to dodge him at the last second.

The dog recovered and looked up adoringly at Mackenzie, who'd been known to slip him forbidden delights during previous visits. His near-hairless body quivered from nose to tail. Without his thick, shaggy coat, the poor thing looked more like a newly shorn sheep than a sheep*dog,* but he was still big enough to knock over a dump truck.

"Downstairs," Adam ordered, pointing to an open door halfway down the hall. Radizwell gave a long, mournful whine.

"Now!"

Throwing piteous looks over his shoulder, the animal plopped down on his belly and inched across the tiles. He paused at the open door, gave another whine and slunk down the stairs.

Mackenzie watched him disappear with some trepidation. She knew the stairs led down to Maggie's luxurious office, where her mentor had just finished revisions to her groundbreaking tome on infant phonetics. She also knew Terence the iguana considered the office his personal domain. Mackenzie only hoped the lizard wasn't currently occupying his favorite perch on Maggie's desk. The horny sheepdog would go nuts trying to get at him.

"Don't worry," Adam said, guessing the direction of her thoughts. "Terence is *up*stairs in the girls' playroom. With the door locked. I promise you and Nick a little peace tonight. As much as you can hope for," he amended, ruffling his eldest daughter's curls, "with this demolitions expert-in-training and her sister to contend with."

Jilly giggled at what she obviously considered a high compliment and raised only a token protest when her father firmly closed the door leading to the basement. The sheepdog was her willing slave. She'd ride his back, dress him in her parents' clothing, spray paint his fur. Tonight, though, she had 'Kenzie to play with. And her uncle Nick.

"Nick and Maggie are in the kitchen," Adam informed Mackenzie. "The unprincipled rogue is seducing my wife with wild mushrooms."

"No, daddy," Jilly protested. "Uncle Nick can't s'duce mommy. She's already got a baby in her tummy. You put it there, remember?"

"As a matter of fact," he replied, grinning at his precocious child, "I do."

Dodging doll carriages, umbrellas and the tumbled plastic walls of a medieval castle, they made their way past an exquisite bombé chest topped by a gilt mirror that had once reflected the image of a Hungarian princess. An inch-thick Aubusson runner in rich ruby tones absorbed their footsteps.

When they entered the kitchen at the rear of the house, laughter drifted out to greet them, along with a host of tantalizing aromas. Even Mackenzie, whose taste ran to pizza, tacos and the occasional well-done rib eye, sniffed appreciatively. Hefting Samantha higher on her hip, she paused to survey the scene.

As always, the warmth and elegance of the kitchen/breakfast room/family area reached out to grab at her heart. It ran the whole back of the house. Tall French doors opened out on an English garden, complete with brick walks, boxwood hedges, glorious roses and a Victorian-style gazebo where the girls held their tea parties.

Inside the kitchen, everything was blue, white and bright, sunshiny yellow. Delftware plates decorated the walls. Colorful chintz covered the seat cushions and draped the windows. Copper glinted, and a large brick fireplace made her long for cold winter nights and a bright, blazing fire.

Someday, Mackenzie thought. Someday maybe she'd have a home like this and bright-eyed imps

like Jilly and Samantha to wrap her arms and her
heart around. And a completely besotted husband
like Adam, whose interests did *not* extend to his
neighbor's wife.

Or to supermodels and movie starlets.

A little crease formed between her brows as her
glance went to the tall, broad-shouldered chef working his magic at the cooking island. Nick had shed
his tie and jacket, but his deep tan, monogrammed
shirt and knife-pleated gray slacks screamed wealth
and sophistication. It was hard to picture him bur-
rowing through mud and under concertina wire to
take down a gunrunner. Harder still to imagine him
giving up his string of pricey restaurants and globe-
trotting lifestyle to become a stay-at-home dad, as
Adam Ridgeway had done the first few years after
Jillian's birth.

Mackenzie could, on the other hand, easily picture him in the role he seemed so well suited for.
If even half the stories in the tabloids were to be
believed, Nick Jensen was a world-class lover.
Every cover girl and screen goddess he'd been
paired with over the years gushed about his seductive charm, his generosity, his solicitous attention.
In *and* out of bed.

Not that she was the least interested in that particular aspect of her boss. Even if she wasn't still
cautious after her divorce, her years in the navy had

conditioned her to avoid anything that smacked of
fooling around within the ranks. She'd have to be
crazy to even *think* about wrestling the man down
to the floor and having her way with him.

Nick looked up at that moment and caught her
frown. "Don't worry, Comm. You'll like it."

For a startled moment, she thought he'd read her
mind. "Huh?"

"The appetizer," he said, nodding to a laden silver tray. "This is my own recipe for sherry mushrooms *en croûte*. You'll like it."

"Don't believe him!"

Maggie rounded the counter. Eight months pregnant and stunning in a floor-length gown of royal
blue, she held out a toothpicked appetizer.

"You'll *love* it! Here, sink your teeth into this."

The featherlight pastry melted on Mackenzie's
tongue. If those were mushrooms inside, they sure
fooled her. The succulent morsels had a dark, rich
flavor she'd never tasted before.

"And to think we'll be dining tonight on under-
cooked prime rib and overcooked broccoli." Sighing, Maggie speared another pastry and popped it
into her mouth.

Nick gave her an amused look. "You should
have convinced the awards committee to hold the
banquet at my restaurant, as I suggested."

"Are you kidding? Despite your offer to feed us

at cost, not even the International Monetary Fund can afford dinner for three hundred at Nick's.''

Adam glanced pointedly at his watch. ''Speaking of the IMF...''

''I'm coming, I'm coming!''

Snagging another of the flaky tidbits, Maggie chewed, swallowed and rattled off last-minute instructions.

''The girls have had their supper and their baths. They'll be ready for bed about the time Nick says your dinner will finish cooking. Jilly's eardrops are on the nightstand beside her bed. One squirt in each ear. Don't let Samantha have any more apple juice. It goes right through her. If Terence gets loose...''

''God help you,'' Adam muttered.

Shooting her husband a quelling look, Maggie grabbed her evening bag. ''We both have our cell phones. Call if you need us. Bye, Nick. Bye, Mackenzie. Bye-bye, sugar pies.''

She planted noisy, smacking kisses on the cheek of each girl. Adam waited patiently, then took his turn. A few minutes later, the garage door rumbled up, then down. Before their vehicle had cleared the front drive, a low, mournful howl drifted up from the basement. Another followed, longer and louder than the first. The third rose to an earsplitting crescendo.

''Radizwell doesn't like it when Mommy and

Daddy go off and leave him in the basement,'' Jilly informed Nick and Mackenzie between yowls. "He can go all night,'' she added with some pride.

"I'd better let him up,'' Nick muttered. "Brace yourself.''

Nodding, Mackenzie plunked Samantha on the countertop and took a wide-legged stance. Nick made sure she was ready before he opened the hall door.

Neither one of them could have known it at the time, but by that simple act he saved both their lives.

Chapter 2

The attack didn't come until almost two hours later.

Looking back, Mackenzie would always marvel at how blissfully unaware she'd been her life was about to take a sharp turn into danger and international intrigue. Nothing in those hours leading up to the murderous assault gave any warning of what was to come.

The time was filled with nothing but noise and laughter. Shrieks of delight as Jilly and Samantha used the family room sofa as a springboard onto Nick's prone body. Loud grunts when they landed feet first on his midsection. Earsplitting protests from Radizwell, who danced around the threesome wanting in on the fun.

Mackenzie kept a wary eye on lamps, books and silver-framed photographs and generally stayed out of the fray. She did, however, get suckered into playing the part of Bad Bunny when Jilly dragged out a set of plush hand puppets and a folding cardboard stage. With the air of a general marshaling her troops, the pint-size director issued orders to her cast and crew.

"You put the stage together, Uncle Nick. Fold the tabs over like this. See?"

"Got it."

"'Kenzie, you sit here. Samantha has to sit in your lap 'cause she's just a baby."

Her sister's rosebud mouth puckered at the disparaging remark. "Nuh-uh."

"Yes, you are. A silly little baby."

Tears welled. A chubby fist closed over a puppet in the shape of a bear. Before Mackenzie could stop her, Samantha swung.

Screeching, Jilly swung back. Radizwell set the windows to rattling with his bark.

It took a moment or two for Nick and Mackenzie to separate the combatants. They emerged from their brawl with sulky expressions that melted instantly into happy smiles when Nick suggested ice cream after they finished their theatrical production.

Finally—*finally!*—eight o'clock rolled around. Breathing a heartfelt sigh of relief, Mackenzie rinsed out the ice-cream bowls while Nick carried Samantha upstairs on his shoulders. Jilly raced ahead to select the books she wanted to read before lights out.

A half hour later, the girls were ear-dropped, pottied, story-taled and snuggled in. Nick dropped kisses on their cheeks and went downstairs to stir his pots, leaving Mackenzie to deposit their various items of discarded clothing in the hamper.

When she opened the door to the bathroom, though, an ominous hissing sound greeted her. Evidently Terence the iguana had heard the sounds of the toilet flushing and decided to migrate from the playroom next door. He had now taken up occupancy in the bathtub.

Radizwell, who'd plopped down beside Jilly's bed, went on full love alert. Hastily, Mackenzie yanked the door shut, separating him from the bug-eyed creature in the tub.

"Sorry," she told the quivering sheepdog. "I don't think he's in the mood for love right now."

She just wished she could say the same!

Only now, with the girls tucked in and Nick downstairs, could she catch her breath and put a name to this tingling, prickly sensation she'd been experiencing for the past few hours. The sensation had intensified each time Nick grinned at the girls' antics. Or sprawled loose-limbed and feigning exhaustion while they climbed all over him. Or solemnly danced his grasshopper hand puppet across the cardboard stage.

Mackenzie had seen a different side of Nick Jensen tonight—gentler, funnier, more relaxed. The disconcerting glimpses of the man behind the handsome mask had totally skewed the image she'd constructed of him over the past years. As OMEGA's chief of communications, she'd monitored Lightning's operations in the field. She knew how good he was. And how lethal.

She'd also monitored his activities when not in the field. It wasn't difficult to keep up with them. The paparazzi followed him like hounds after a sleek, handsome fox. According to the tabloids' various "reliable sources," he could have his pick of the half-dozen gorgeous beauties reportedly madly in love with him.

Although…

Mackenzie could have sworn she'd caught a speculative gleam in his eyes when he looked at her lately. Part of her wanted to believe it telegraphed a very definite male interest. The rest of her got clammy at the thought.

Nick Jensen was out of her league. Correction, out of her universe. And despite the fact he'd spent hours tussling with kids and their near hairless sheepdog on the floor, she'd be a fool to believe he possessed any more homing instincts than her philandering ex.

Or so she tried to convince herself as she and Radizwell made their way downstairs.

Seeing Nick in his natural habitat didn't exactly reinforce her theory. He looked right at home at the stove, darn him! Far more than Mackenzie herself did on the rare occasions she attempted anything more esoteric than nachos or microwave popcorn. He'd even set the table. Candles flickered amid the blue-and-white crockery and tall-stemmed cobalt goblets.

"Almost ready," he assured her.

"I know it's a little late to ask, but what can I do to help?"

"Why don't you do the honors with the wine? I uncorked it but was waiting for you to come down before pouring."

Extracting the bottle from the crystal ice bucket, Mackenzie gave its label a curious glance. "Mt. Blaze?"

"It's a small vineyard on New Zealand's Gold Coast. Their late-harvest Riesling won *Wine Enthusiast*'s best vintage award three years running."

"Oooh-kay."

Detouring around the recumbent sheepdog, Mackenzie brought two filled goblets to the cooking island. "What shall we drink to?"

Nick swirled the pale liquid, savoring its light, fruity bouquet. His glance caught hers.

Dammit, there it was again! That indecipherable look. The message she couldn't quite interpret. Mackenzie's breath hitched and that damned jittery sensation returned with a vengeance.

"How about our first dinner together?" he suggested.

How about their *last!*

She wasn't a fool. Or dead from the neck down. She could recognize healthy, old-fashioned lust when it shivered through her. She just wasn't ready to deal with it.

"To dinner," she echoed faintly.

He clinked her glass softly, took a sip and turned back to the stove to stir a thick, creamy sauce.

Mackenzie blew out a slow breath. Maybe he hadn't noticed that little blip on her internal radar screen. Sliding one hip onto a cane-backed stool, she eyed the slowly bubbling froth he was stirring.

"What's that?"

"Béchamel."

"And béchamel is?"

"A seafood-based white sauce used in a number of Mediterranean dishes. I seem to remember promising you the real thing a few weeks ago."

He had, she remembered. Right after hand-delivering one of the countless pizzas she'd ordered while working late at the control center.

"Want a taste?"

Mackenzie studied the little blobs in the sauce with something less than enthusiasm. She wasn't averse to trying new dishes. She merely preferred to have a general idea what they were first. Still, he *had* gone to all this trouble to cook for her. The least she could do was be gracious.

"Sure."

Tearing off a crust of bread, Nick dipped it in the sauce. Mackenzie gave the lumps another doubtful look, but leaned forward to accept the offering.

The bread was warm and fragrant, the sauce a heavenly blend of cream, butter, garlic and shallots. The rubbery lumps took a bit of chewing, but their delicate fish taste wasn't too bad. Not too bad at all.

"What do you think?"

"I think," she announced, swiping her tongue along her lower lip, "I'm better off not knowing what I just ate."

Laughter glinted in his eyes. "Coward."

Her stomach did a little flip that had nothing to do with fishy blobs.

"You've got sauce on your chin."

The glint in his eyes deepened. So did the timbre of his voice.

"I'll get it."

Before she could reach for the blue-and-white towel on the counter, he had it in hand and came around the end of the counter. She swiveled toward him, her back to the tiles, her knees bumping his thigh. Curling a knuckle under her chin, he tilted her face to his.

The gentle swipe of the dish towel raised goose bumps on Mackenzie's skin. The brush of Nick's firm, warm hand against her chin left her fighting to remember all the reasons why she'd decided not to jump his bones.

He was so close Mackenzie could see the gold tips to his lashes. So near she could feel his breath warm on her face. Her heart hammered. Her lips parted.

His thumb traced a slow circle on the side of her chin. The light, lazy touch set every one of her nerves to jumping. She knew she had to pull back, laugh off this crazy moment, or she'd do something monumentally stupid. Like flinging her arms around the man's neck and attacking the mouth so tantalizingly close to her own.

"Nick…"

"Mmm?"

"I, uh, don't think…"

"What?"

"This isn't…"

Radizwell gave a low growl. The rumble barely penetrated Mackenzie's whirling senses but Nick lifted his head and glanced over her shoulder. The next instant, he threw the dish towel aside and wrapped his right fist around her upper arm like a vise.

"Hey!"

"Get down!"

With a violent tug, he yanked her off the bar stool and threw her behind the counter. He followed her down. They hit the tiles a mere second before the wall of windows overlooking the garden exploded in a burst of glass and gunfire.

Bullets ripped into walls, cabinets, appliances. Raked the table, shattering dishes. Slammed into the stove. Sent boiling white sauce spraying.

Crushed against the floor tile by Nick's weight, Mackenzie couldn't breathe, couldn't move. The stuttering gunfire seemed to go on for two lifetimes. Burst after burst. Deafening. Terrifying.

Suddenly, there was silence. Blessed silence. For a heartbeat, maybe two. Then glass crunched and she heard the thud of running feet.

Nick rolled off her, sprang up. Mackenzie scrabbled onto her knees, trying frantically to get her feet under her. She lifted her head just in time to see

Nick's arm whip forward. A long-bladed kitchen knife flew across the room.

She heard an agonized scream. Another burst of gunfire. A feral snarl. Fangs bared, Radizwell streaked past her.

"Arrrgh!"

Bullets plowed into the ceiling, traced a wild pattern across plaster. Huge chunks rained down.

Nick leaped over the counter. Mackenzie raced around it a second later, horrified by the sight of Radizwell savaging a screaming, writhing figure dressed all in black. She was even more horrified when she saw the bastard still gripped his Uzi with one hand. He kept firing wild bursts while he tried desperately to fight off the dog with his other arm.

All Mackenzie could think of, all that pierced her frantic thoughts, was that the girls were asleep upstairs. Right above them. The stream of bullets could penetrate the flooring, plow through their mattresses.

Nick must have had the same gripping fear. His foot swung in a savage arc. The Uzi went flying. Only then did he attempt to drag Radizwell off the screaming victim. He got a fist around the dog's collar and heaved.

Radizwell reared back, but was only gathering his muscles for another attack. Fangs bared, claws scrabbling on the tiles, he lunged forward once

more. His size and fury carried Nick with him. The
man on the floor frantically crabbed backward,
kicking at Nick, at the dog, managing to get free of
both. His hand went to his underarm holster.

Mackenzie didn't stop to think, didn't calculate
the odds. She dived for the Uzi, got her hands
around the grip at the same instant the bastard in
black leveled a .9mm Beretta.

He pumped out one shot, only one, before she
fired.

Chapter 3

The D.C. fire department, the police department's crime scene unit, several detectives and a squad from the coroner's office were already at the house when Maggie and Adam rushed in. Face ashen, Maggie took in the black plastic body bags on the kitchen floor. Her eyes were haunted as they locked on Nick.

"Samantha? Jilly? You said on the phone…" Her voice cracked, broke. "They're okay?"

"They're fine."

Nick's shoes crunched on broken glass as he crossed the kitchen and gripped both her hands in his.

"They were in bed, asleep. Jilly didn't wake up until she heard the sirens. Samantha stayed down for the entire count."

"A police officer is upstairs with them now," Mackenzie put in. "We figured we'd better have someone keep them company until, well…"

She glanced at Adam. His jaw was set, his blue eyes arctic. He didn't exude the charm of a handsome, wealthy Boston aristocrat now. He was Thunder, once OMEGA's most skilled, dangerous agent.

"Until we figure out who was behind the attack," Adam finished in a voice so soft and lethal it sent shivers down Mackenzie's spine.

The idea that her children might need guarding in their own home drained the little color remaining in Maggie's cheeks.

"I have to see them," she got out. "Make sure they're okay."

Adam went upstairs with her. When they came back downstairs a short time later, Maggie's face reflected the same savage determination as her husband's.

"What have we got so far?"

"Two corpses," Nick replied succinctly. "No identification on either. A near arsenal of weapons, all of which appear to have been stolen. A very sophisticated, very expensive electronic security bypass device. If Radizwell hadn't heard them outside in the garden and given us a half-second warning..."

At the sound of his name, the sheepdog's tail thumped the floor. Adam reached down to scratch behind his ear.

"You've just earned yourself a year's worth of T-bones, pal. And free run of the house for the rest of your life."

"Jilly will be happy to hear that," Mackenzie said with her first smile since the bullets had started flying. Only now was the knot at the base of her skull beginning to loosen.

It kinked up again when the squad from the coroner's office lifted the two corpses onto gurneys and wheeled them out. The carving knife that had gone through the throat of one of the gunmen tented his plastic body bag at neck level.

Adam's glance sliced to Nick. "Your handiwork?"

"Yes. Mackenzie got the second bastard."

"Good work, Mac."

She accepted quiet words of praise with a small nod. She wasn't one of OMEGA's highly skilled field operatives, but she'd gone through enough training to hold her own in a tight situation. Hopefully, she'd never find herself in one *this* tight again!

"Mr. Ridgeway? Dr. Sinclair?"

Maggie and Adam turned to the two detectives, who introduced themselves and produced their credentials. The older and the paunchier of the two addressed Adam.

"I understand you were supposed to receive an award tonight."

"That's correct."

"Was the award publicized?"

"There was mention of it in most of the papers."

"And on local TV stations," Maggie added.

The younger detective jotted the information down in his notebook.

"Are you assuming the gunmen knew my wife and I weren't home?" Adam asked, eyes narrowed.

"We're not assuming anything right now. Just getting the facts."

Adam shared a glance with his wife. Mackenzie could see they were beginning to work through the possibilities she and Nick had been discussing since their hearts stopped pumping pure adrenaline and their brains reengaged.

If the attack was specifically timed for after Adam and Maggie left, the gunmen might have been intending to take the girls for ransom. Or exact vengeance against Maggie and/or Adam by destroying their home and family. God knew, both Chameleon and Thunder had taken down their share of scum in their days with OMEGA. Any one of those bastards could have been seeking retribution.

Then again, their target might not have been the girls at all. The gunmen might have been after Nick. Or Mackenzie.

The idea made her swallow. Hard.

She knew they wouldn't narrow the possibilities until the coroner autopsied the bodies, the police followed up on every lead and OMEGA put its vast resources to work. Mackenzie suspected she had access to more databases than every city, state and Federal agency combined. She'd soon know if either of the scum who burst in tonight with guns blazing had been fingerprinted, DNA tested, given blood or peed into a cup any time in the past twenty years.

They hadn't.

At least not that Mackenzie could determine. Once she received the autopsy results and crime scene analysis, she spent two frustrating days crossmatching the information with medical, dental and Red Cross databanks. At the same time, she followed convoluted trails to determine the source of both the gunmen's weapons and clothing.

The first solid break came not from bodily fluids, fiber content or serial numbers, but from the trash littering the back seat of a nondescript gray sedan found abandoned a block or so from Maggie and Adam's house. The vehicle had been reported stolen weeks ago in Atlanta. The license plates were also hot. But the back seat yielded a veritable treasure trove.

By running the list of fast-food containers and crumpled coffee cups through her computers, Mackenzie was able to plot all franchises selling those products within a fifty-mile radius of D.C. She then suggested the detectives handling the case e-mail pictures of the gunmen to the managers of each franchise. Within twenty-four hours from the time the car was found, they'd established a pattern that centered on Nick.

The gunmen had purchased donuts at a Krispy Kreme three blocks from his house. Bought chili dogs from a vendor located across the street from his pricey restaurant in Chevy Chase. Downed cup after cup of coffee from a Starbucks on Massachusetts Avenue, just around the corner from the Offices of the Special Envoy.

"According to one of the waitresses at this Starbucks," Mackenzie told Nick in a voice laced with satisfaction, "they made a call on the pay phone located on the premises the morning of the attack."

Plunking down a list, she hitched a hip on the corner of his desk. She hadn't bothered with makeup this morning. She rarely did. But the way

Nick's glance shifted when she crossed her legs made her wonder why the heck she'd opted for a white blouse and a slim black skirt with a slit on one side instead of her usual slacks.

Ha! Who was she kidding? She knew why. That damned almost-kiss.

To her consternation, Mackenzie had relived those absurd moments just before the gunmen struck too many times for her own comfort the past few days. Just thinking about the way Nick's mouth had hovered over hers got her all flustered. And irritated.

Particularly since Nick hadn't appeared to have spared those breathless moments a second thought. Like Mackenzie, he'd devoted every hour not taken up with his social obligations as special envoy and his duties as OMEGA director to discovering who was behind the attack. She didn't know how he could work such long hours, juggling so many roles, and look like he'd just stepped out of the pages of *GQ*. Not even Ace's secure satellite transmission from Saudi a while ago, reporting another dead end on the oil refinery sabotage, had ruffled his composure.

Nor should Mackenzie let him ruffle hers. This was Lightning, for pity's sake! Her boss. The man she'd sensed could be trouble since her first day at OMEGA. If she had half a brain in her head, she'd go hard astern and put plenty of blue water between them before she made a fool of herself. Again!

Frowning, Mackenzie uncrossed her legs and gave him a rundown on the list. "These are all calls made from the Starbucks the day of the attack. I've crossed through the numbers that check to friends or relatives of employees. The rest appear to be calls to doctors' offices, dry cleaners and the like. All except this one. Europol's running it now."

Nick eyed the number. He didn't need the European Police Office's aid to identify the country code. It was as familiar to him as his own name.

"The south of France," he murmured. "From the area designation, I'd say the call was made to the Riviera."

"You nailed it. It went to a phone booth in the city of Nice, to be exact."

Images of an azure sea lapping a broad boardwalk and a flower market filled with riotous color flashed into Nick's mind. He'd only visited Nice a few times. He'd always found the pickings in Cannes to be more than sufficient for his needs.

"It's beginning to look like someone in Nice wants you dead," Mackenzie commented, studying his face intently. "Any idea who?"

"No, but I certainly intend to find out. Ask Mrs. Wells to come in on your way out, please. I'll get her working on travel arrangements, then come upstairs and brief you on the operations I want you to track while I'm gone.''

The vertical line between Mackenzie's brows deepened. Not two seconds ago, she'd made up her mind to put some blue water between her and Nick. Not, however, an entire ocean. And not when it came to finding out why those bastards had opened fire on her.

''You're not thinking about jetting off to France without me, are you?''

''There's no thinking about it.''

Leaning back in his chair, he smoothed a hand down his red-and-navy striped tie. His nails were neat and trimmed, Mackenzie noted, his wrist banded by a thin gold watch. For all his reputed wealth, Nick didn't go for big or flashy. The memory of how those strong, sure fingers had grazed her chin deepened her frown into a near scowl. Or maybe it was how close their mouths had come to doing a little grazing of their own.

''You weren't the only one shot at,'' she pointed out. ''I have a personal stake in finding out who hired those thugs, too.''

''The evidence seems to indicate I was the target.''

''*Seems* being the operative word.''

Pushing away from his desk, Mackenzie paced

the plush Turkish carpet. She'd done a lot of thinking in the past twenty-four hours.

"I did a Mediterranean cruise with the Sixth Fleet during my navy days. We home-ported in Naples, and I took a couple of shore leaves up along the Italian Riviera. Never got to Nice, but it's only a hop, skip and a jump from San Remo. Maybe I saw something I wasn't supposed to see. Maybe I listened in on some ship-to-ship communications I wasn't supposed to hear. This could be about me, Nick, not you."

"The surveillance pattern you established for the two gunmen says otherwise."

"I think I should go with you."

He shook his head. "I work alone. I always have. Besides, you're not trained for field operations."

"Tell that to the guy at the morgue."

The swift comeback earned her a hard look. Mackenzie took it without a blink. Roles and missions had become something of a sore point between her and Nick since that operation in San Antonio some months back. She really couldn't understand why he still got steamed over the fact that she'd snuggled up to the country club type who'd hired a hit man to kidnap and kill his wife. Helping take the sleazy contractor down had provided Mackenzie intense satisfaction. It was hard to accept being relegated to mere staff work again.

Which was where Nick seemed determined to keep her.

Rising with the fluid, pantherlike grace that characterized him, he rounded the desk. Mackenzie found herself trapped between a solid block of mahogany and one hundred eighty-plus pounds of lean muscle encased in a hand-tailored Brioni suit.

"One of the first rules of survival in the field is to avoid unnecessary distractions. And you, Comm, are in serious danger of becoming a distraction."

Mackenzie waffled between feeling flattered and insulted for all of two seconds before deciding on insulted. She'd experienced plenty of sexism in the navy, some unintentional, some not. She hadn't put up with it then. She wasn't about to now. In her characteristic way, she laid the matter right on the line.

"If you're referring to how close we came to a lip-lock the other night, we both know it wouldn't have happened. Neither one of us is the type to indulge in an office affair."

He cocked his head, measuring her through a screen of ridiculously sexy gold-tipped lashes. "You're sure about that?"

"Yes." She looked him square in the eye. "I'm

sure. You're a professional, Nick. You take your work very seriously. So do I. I could send one of my technicians over to work communications for you, but I prefer to go myself. Like you, I've got a score to settle with whoever hired those bastards. And we both know I'm the best in the business when it comes to comm.''

She was. Nick couldn't argue that. In all his years with OMEGA, he'd never encountered anyone with anything close to this woman's uncanny ability. She could coax a signal from a dead satellite or milk data from supposedly secure, protected sources. He'd also spent enough years in the field to know how vital good comm was. You never knew when you might need an alternate escape route or an emergency on-scene extraction.

But his gut still kinked whenever he remembered how close Mackenzie had come to taking a bullet the other night. Everything in him shied away from the idea of putting her in the line of fire again.

For the first time since taking over as OMEGA's acting director he understood how Adam Ridgeway must have felt whenever Maggie went into the field. Sending men and women you considered your friends into harm's way was gut-clenching enough. Sending the stubborn, irritating female who'd somehow managed to get under his skin was infinitely worse.

The only plus that Nick could see to taking her to Nice with him was that he could keep an eye on her. They were both operating under the assumption that he was the target, but, as Mackenzie had pointed out, they hadn't nailed that down yet. They wouldn't until he worked out this French connection. Nick couldn't discount the possibility that she'd been the intended victim, that someone who knew her connection to OMEGA wanted to eliminate her. Or, as she'd suggested, maybe the attack stemmed from her days in the navy.

"All right. I'll have Mrs. Wells reserve two seats on the Concorde, with connecting flights to Nice. We can leave early tomorrow morning and be there in time for dinner. In the meantime..."

His glance roamed her neat white blouse and slim skirt. They represented a significant departure from her usual jeans but wouldn't hack it at one of the most exclusive resorts on the Côte d'Azur.

"Get the Field Dress unit to fix you up with a wardrobe. You'd better take several gowns, a couple of cocktail dresses, a selection of resort daywear. And bikinis. You'll only need the bottoms, of course."

"Of course."

Mackenzie didn't bat an eye. She knew from her Mediterranean cruise that everyone went topless on European beaches except prudish, self-conscious American tourists. No way she was going to admit she'd fallen smack into the prude category.

"We'll stay at the Negresco," Nick told her. "The owner has put out tentative feelers about the possibility of opening a Nick's at the hotel. That will give me the perfect cover for a visit."

"What about my cover?"

He made a show of shooting his snowy cuffs and Mackenzie guessed immediately what was coming. The man had a tabloid reputation to live up to, after all.

"The best cover is always the simplest. When asked, we'll merely introduce you as my companion."

"Define companion."

"Friend. Mistress. Lover."

"I don't think so," Mackenzie drawled. "Let's go with business associate."

For the first time since the attack, real amusement flickered in Nick's eyes. "Do you really think the French will make any distinction between the two?"

"The French might not, but we will."

* * *

With that firm pronouncement, Mackenzie left his office and plunged into her own preparations for the mission. Her first stop was the control center, where she had the communications tech on duty call in the rest of her crew. While waiting for them to arrive, she zapped out a few queries and began compiling a complete social, economic and geopolitical history of the French Riviera in general and the city of Nice in particular.

That done, she zipped down to the basement and consulted the magicians in Field Dress Unit. Field Dress had more experience outfitting OMEGA's agents with Kevlar body armor, jungle fatigues and the latest in Arctic survival gear than designer originals. But as soon as Mackenzie explained her needs, the frizzy-haired genius who headed the unit sent his team to scour Washington's most elite boutiques.

Within hours they'd decked Mackenzie out in sinfully decadent silk lingerie, the latest fall lines from Versace and Armani, shoes by Ferragamo, and handbags from Prada and Chanel. As Nick's "associate," she had to exude at least a degree of the same wealth and sophistication he did.

If an entire new wardrobe wasn't enough to make her feel like Sandra Bullock in *Miss Congeniality II,* the haughty, self-important genius Field Dress brought in to tame her shoulder-length mane would have done the trick. As Mackenzie explained to the stylist, she usually just twisted the mink-brown mass at the back of her head, anchored it with a plastic clip, and went about her business.

"Obviously," the artist sniffed.

When finally released from Field Dress, a gelled, manicured and pedicured Mackenzie escaped to control center. Her communications technicians greeted her with a barrage of grins and wolf whistles.

"Whoooo-weee!" the oldest of the group exclaimed. "That's some new look, boss."

Mackenzie tossed her head, flipping a glossy swirl over one shoulder, and returned John's grin.

"Like it?"

"What's not to like?"

She'd worked with the happily married father of four long enough now to accept the compliment as intended.

"You may change your mind when you realize we have to stuff a suitcase load of electronics into this little number," she told him, dangling her Prada handbag by its strap.

Her group of experts instantly focused on the envelope-size bag. There was nothing they loved more than a challenge like this one.

"Good thing we've acquired those new, miniaturized circuit boards," John murmured. "What are you thinking you'll need, chief?"

Mackenzie had worked the list in her mind while Field Dress attacked her body. She had no idea what she and Lightning might run into in France, but she intended to be prepared for just about anything.

"I want secure satellite voice transmitters for both me and Lightning, NAVSAT directional finders, biochemical sensors, a sound amplifier that will let me listen to conversations up to fifty meters away and the sharpest high-resolution surveillance cameras in our inventory. Plus the new Taser we've been testing."

John gave another whistle. The Taser was the latest CIA version of a stun gun. No larger than an ordinary ballpoint pen, it packed a powerful punch. A quarter-second contact caused instantaneous muscle contraction. One to two seconds short-circuited an attacker's neuro-centers and brought him down. Three would leave him staring at the ceiling in a daze.

Given that an agent's life could well depend on the equipment he or she took into the field, Mackenzie and her people thoroughly tested every device they added to their electronic grab bag. She and John had both endured only a half-second zap. That was more than enough to convince both of them of the effectiveness of this particular device.

"Hope you don't have to use that baby in an operational mode," John commented, remembering how he'd snarled like a bear with a sore paw for days after the test.

"Not to worry," Mackenzie returned with a shrug. "I'll save it for the bad guys."

Chapter 4

Mackenzie and Nick left for the Riviera early the next morning. She'd never flown aboard the Concorde before and firmly squelched memories of its horrible crash outside Paris some years ago. The sleek, needle-nosed jet represented the ultimate in luxury and speed. A three-and-a-half hour transatlantic flight took them into Paris, where a short connecting flight ferried them to the south of France.

Given the five-hour time difference, Mackenzie and Nick stepped out of the Nice airport into a late afternoon drenched with the scent of honeysuckle and bougainvillea. She pushed her Chanel sunglasses up the top of her head and breathed in the perfumed air. With it came a pungent tang that mariners the world over immediately recognized.

The sea was close, so close she could almost taste its salt. She was still savoring the familiar scent when Nick slid a hand under her arm and guided her toward the mile-long limo idling at the curb. Its short, stocky uniformed chauffeur jumped to attention at their approach.

"*Bonjour,* Monsieur Jensen. I am Jean-Claude Broussard, your driver. Welcome to Nice."

"*Merci. Je suis très heureux d'être de retour.*"

The reply earned Nick a look of respect from the chauffeur and a curious glance from Mackenzie. She knew Lightning had been born somewhere in France, but that's all she or anyone else at OMEGA knew about his life before he was adopted by Paige and Doc Jensen and brought to the States. He'd grown up in California, graduated from Stanford and joined OMEGA not long after a tour in the military. In all the time Mackenzie had worked with him, he'd never used any gestures or slang that would mark him as anything but American.

Yet she'd sensed the change in him almost from the moment the Concorde had touched down in Paris. He seemed more casual, yet somehow more cosmopolitan. As if he were changing his spots to suit his environment. A leopard blending into the dry, brown African veld.

Only this veld wasn't dry *or* brown. As the limo rolled out of the airport and sped past the more industrial areas, a landscape filled with brilliant color began to unfold. Red-tile-roofed villas stair-stepped down sheer cliffs. Palm trees waved lacy fronds against the early evening sky. Orange and pink and purple blossoms climbed walls, spilled from flower boxes, twined along wrought iron balconies.

And the Mediterranean! She'd forgotten how beautiful—and changeable—it was. At its deepest, the waters were a dark, unfathomable navy. Here, closer to land, waves of alternating shades of turquoise, lapis and aquamarine teased the shore. Sighing at the sight, Mackenzie used the drive in from the airport to reset her mental clock and run through the data she'd pulled up about Nice.

Native Ligurians had occupied the steep hills above the sea for thousands of years before conquering Greeks established the "modern" city of Nikaia on the site. The Romans followed the Greeks, constructing a forum, extensive baths and an amphitheater. In medieval times, rival armies from Provence, Tuscany, Savoy and Turkey all battled over the city at various times, until the French finally took permanent possession.

The next invasion occurred during the Belle Epoque of the late 1800s, when Nice became a fashionable winter retreat for aristocrats from all over Europe. Queen Victoria visited regularly. So did the Tsar and Tsarina of Russia. The onion-shaped domes of the cathedral they'd built in honor of their oldest son, who died suddenly of an illness while vacationing in Nice, were just visible over the sea of red-tiled roofs.

Along with the rich and titled came the artists and actors. Matisse lived and painted here until his death in 1954. Picasso, Dali, Chagall were all seduced by the dazzling light and shimmering colors of the coast. F. Scott Fitzgerald and his wife Zelda held court at their favorite table in the Negresco. Rudolph Valentino, Maurice Chevalier, Marlene Dietrich, and Gary Cooper, to name just a few, strolled the Promenade des Anglais, named for the English visitors whose wealth brought such prosperity to the little seaside resort.

Nice was just as popular today as it had been at the turn of the century. With neighboring Cannes only a few miles to the east and the principality of Monaco just around the bay to the west, new royalty in the form of rock stars and sports figures now patronized its very exclusive and very expensive boutiques.

No computer-generated report could prepare Mackenzie for the actual impact of the famous resort, however. Lowering the shaded window, she gawked like any tourist as the limo swept down the Promenade des Anglais. Hotels and palaces bordered one side of the broad, palm-lined thoroughfare, the Mediterranean the other.

This was the famous boulevard where aristocrats once paraded beneath straw boaters and lacy parasols. Where the eccentric American dancer, Isadora Duncan, choked to death in 1927, when her long scarf caught under the wheel of her automobile as it sped along the promenade. Where lovers of all ages still strolled hand in hand.

The sun worshippers were out in full force on the pebbled beaches, soaking up the slanting rays in blue-painted wooden beach chairs. A good many of the women, Mackenzie noted, had opted for bottomless as well as topless. Heads tipped back, legs outstretched, hands clasped over their bare middles, they indulged in the serious business of doing nothing.

Sunbathers weren't the only ones enjoying the golden glow cast over the sea. Yachts and cabin cruisers of every size bobbed in the exclusive marinas sprinkled along the promenade. Bikini-clad nymphs and paunchy boat owners in *Zorba the Greek* hats lounged on the aft decks, sipping aperitifs. Larger craft drifted at the ends of their anchor chains farther out on the bay.

Halfway down the Promenade des Anglais the

marble statue of a large woman in what looked like peasant dress sat perched atop a tall column. Leaning forward, Mackenzie squinted up at the curious figure.

"Who's that?" she asked the driver through the Plexiglas divider.

"Ahhh, that one." Jean-Claude kissed his fingertips to the statue. "She is the patron saint of our city. A laundress who saves Nice from the Turks many, many years ago." He grinned at his passengers via the rearview mirror. "She is fat, no?"

"Well…"

"And ugly. So very ugly."

Mackenzie had to admit the woman wouldn't win any beauty contests. With her fleshy jowls, overlapping chins and great, humped nose, she scared off even the pigeons. Jean-Claude seemed to take great pride in her repulsiveness.

"When the Turks come," he explained, "this laundress climbs to the city wall. She bends over, lifts her skirt, and wiggles her so fat, so bare… Uh… How do you say…?"

"Derriere," Nick supplied dryly.

"*Mais oui!* Her derriere. The Turks, they take one look and retreat immediately. The laundress, she becomes our patron saint."

Laughing, Mackenzie snuggled back against the leather. She wasn't sure whether to believe the outrageous tale, but the idea that the citizens of Nice would erect a monument to the woman who mooned an invading army gave her a whole different perspective on the city and its people. The Niçois, it appeared, had a lively sense of humor.

She was still chuckling as the limo glided to a stop at their hotel. When the driver handed her out, she couldn't hold back a gasp at its turn-of-the-century splendor.

"C'est magnifique, oui?" Jean-Claude asked, beaming with proprietary pride.

"And then some."

A monstrous copper-topped dome crowned the hotel's corner entrance. Elaborate mansards decorated the wings that swept out to either side. The gleaming white marble structure had to take up a full city block! The interior beckoned through revolving brass-and-glass doors, as plush and Victorian as the exterior.

Leaving the chauffeur and bellman to attend to the luggage, Nick slid a hand under Mackenzie's elbow and escorted her inside. His touch was light and just casual enough to raise little goose bumps all up and down her arm.

For Pete's sake! She had to get a grip here.

She was the one who'd argued her way into this mission. She'd insisted the little interlude between her and Nick a few nights ago didn't mean anything, that they were both professional enough to separate business from pleasure. Still, she couldn't help remembering his cynical remark that the French didn't differentiate between the business associate and the mistress of a virile and very wealthy executive. As if to prove his point, the hotel manager gave her an admiring once-over before turning to Nick with a look that conveyed approval, deference and just a touch of envy.

"Welcome back to the Negresco, Monsieur Jensen. I hope your drive in from the airport was pleasant."

"Very."

In his old-fashioned cutaway jacket and ascot of gray striped silk, the manager carried himself with a dignity worthy of an establishment that ranked among the world's most exclusive hotels. He accepted Nick and Mackenzie's passports with a small bow and snapped his fingers. The clerk behind the counter rushed forward with an envelope containing electronic key cards.

"Your suite is ready," the manager informed them. "Will you wish to have dinner at the hotel this evening? If so, I'll reserve a table for you. We're past high season, you understand, but still…"

He lifted his shoulders in the universal Gallic

shrug that could convey anything from sympathetic understanding to utter contempt.

"We'll dine out tonight," Nick replied. "Mademoiselle Blair wishes to stretch her legs and explore the city a bit."

What Mademoiselle Blair wished was to get the lay of the land. She'd studied satellite images and detailed maps, but the maze of narrow alleys and winding streets in the old part of the city defied any rational layout. Until she walked them and got a feel for their twists and turns, she'd be as lost as any tourist.

They were shown to a penthouse suite filled with antiques that might have graced a duke's palace. Most were from what Nick described as Napoleon's Imperial era. A portrait of the emperor and Josephine in full court regalia stared down from above a marble fireplace that could have easily roasted a buffalo. Gold candelabra inlaid with lapis lazuli framed the portrait.

The central sitting room opened directly onto a terraced balcony that offered a panoramic view of the wide, curving bay. Awed by the glorious spectacle, Mackenzie followed Nick back into the suite to explore the two bedrooms.

He gave her first choice. She didn't hesitate. Greedily, she staked a claim to the one on the left, furnished with a massive sleigh bed crowned by rose-colored brocade bed-hangings. The bed's majesty was impressive enough, but it was the claw-foot bathtub that had her salivating. The thing looked like it could sleep three comfortably.

Shooting the tub a look of intense longing, Mackenzie changed into more casual clothes and rejoined Nick. He'd changed, too, and looked right at home in tan slacks, a pale blue open-necked shirt and a navy blazer with gold monogrammed buttons.

"Give me twenty minutes," Mackenzie said as she unpacked her electronic grab bag. "I want to secure the suite before we go out. Just to make sure we don't come home to any uninvited, gun-toting guests."

Nick had spent enough years in the field to be intimately familiar with most of the equipment she installed. With his assistance, she inserted scramblers into each of the suite's phones to defeat any outside eavesdropping. She then set up active and passive intrusion detection devices and mounted hidden surveillance cameras both in the suite and in the private elevator that accessed it. That done, she suggested a voice check.

"I know we checked the transmitters out before we left Washington, but one more time won't hurt."

Nodding, Nick extracted a solid silver business card case from his blazer's breast pocket. The transmitter embedded in the case was programmed to recognize his voice and activated only when he spoke the code words he himself reprogrammed at will.

"Huckleberry Finn."

Mackenzie's brows rose. Nick grinned and looked like he was going to offer an explanation when a voice floated out of his card case.

"Control here, Lightning. Go ahead."

"Just doing a voice check, Control."

"We read you loud and clear."

"Comm's going to call in next."

"Roger that."

Mackenzie's communications device operated the same way. She murmured two words just loud enough to be picked up by the transmitter fitted into a thin silver bangle bracelet.

"Comm here. How's it going, John?"

"It's going," her second in command replied laconically. "You all settled in Nice?"

"Pretty much. We're going out to get a feel for the streets."

"Roger, Comm. Set your transmitter to track mode and we'll follow you."

With a press of the bracelet's clasp, Mackenzie switched the signal to silent transmit. Then she and Nick left the hotel to stroll through the narrow, cobbled lanes of Vieille Ville, the Old Town. Nick said little, allowing her to record her own impressions.

After three turns, she gave up any idea of navigating these streets on her own. The whole area was a rabbit warren of medieval structures crowded shoulder-to-shoulder, many leaning crookedly, all topped with red tile roofs. Every alley was steeped in the scents of garlic and dank stone.

Only the squares and parks bursting with fountains and flowers allowed her to take a fix on the fold-out map she'd tucked in her purse. At the far end of a long, narrow park, Nick checked the street signs and nodded to a kiosk covered with colorful posters advertising Martini & Rossi vermouth.

"That's the phone."

Mackenzie's stomach tightened. According to Europol, the gunmen who had assaulted her and Nick in Washington had placed a call to this particular pay phone the morning of the attack. The international police agency had e-mailed digitized photos of the kiosk along with its exact location. They'd also mounted a surveillance camera on the two-story brick building facing the kiosk. Mackenzie searched the elaborate facade until she caught the glint of metal, then swept her glance up and down the street to fix the location in her mind.

Not that it would do her much good. Europol had been monitoring the kiosk ever since the attack, photographing every user and running them through their databases. So far, none had turned up any connection, however remote, to Nick.

"What do we do now?"

He tucked her arm in his. "Just what we are doing. Stroll the streets. Watch the sunset from the Promenade des Anglais. Word will get around soon enough that I'm here."

The arrogance of that casual statement would have made Mackenzie blink if she didn't suspect it was true. Although Nice was the fifth largest city in France, it didn't have the frantic beat of a major metropolitan center. As the September evening deepened to a balmy purple dusk, the camera-laden tourists returned to their buses, metallic shutters rolled down over the shop windows and the Niçois themselves took to the sidewalks. Like Nick and Mackenzie, they strolled arm in arm, nodding to acquaintances, exchanging pleasantries, filling the corner bakeries, boulangiers and bars. Patrons gathered at tiny tables to sip aperitifs and punctuate their lively conversation with lively gestures.

By the time Nick and Mackenzie returned to the broad promenade fronting the sea, the sun had dropped below the horizon and it was impossible to tell where the Mediterranean stopped and the night sky began. Out on the bay, strings of lights winked from the yachts riding at anchor.

"I thought we would eat at one of the local bistros tonight. Give you a sample of basic Niçois fare before trying their haute cuisine."

"As long as the sauce doesn't have rubbery little blobs floating around in it, I'm game. Lead the way, skipper."

Nick chose a narrow, two-story restaurant facing the sea. Downstairs, smoke from unfiltered cigarettes blued the air around locals hunched over glasses of wine and anisette, a potent aperitif with the tang of licorice and the wallop of a spooked mule. Upstairs, tall windows opened onto the night. Blue-checkered cloths covered the tables, and an accordion player squeezed out a haunting rendition of "La Vie En Rose."

A waiter with a cigarette tucked behind one ear and a stubby pencil behind the other showed them to a table wedged onto the narrow balcony. Nick translated the day's specials, which turned out to be fish, fish and more fish. Mackenzie ordered grilled sea bass and salad Niçoise. Nick chose a ratatouille, which was some kind of a vegetable medley, and fried squid. While they dipped chunks of crusty bread in a paste made of oil, garlic, capers and chopped olives, she forced herself to shut out the haunting music, the seductive breeze and the lights twinkling out in the bay.

"What's the plan?" she asked quietly. "Surely you have more in mind than just seeing and being seen."

Nick broke off another crust of bread, keeping his expression bland and his thoughts well hidden. He planned to do more than stroll around Nice, all right. A lot more. But he wasn't prepared to read Mackenzie in on his plans.

As he'd pointed out back in Washington, he worked alone. He always had, from his earliest days on the streets right on up through his years with OMEGA. He'd learned early in life that survival often depended on his ability to move quickly, without encumbrances, and keeping his mouth shut. Adding to his inbred caution was the fact that he didn't know who or what he was dealing with. Until he did, he wouldn't put Mackenzie any more at risk than he already had.

He knew better than to voice that thought, however. His chief of communications already considered him several degrees to the right of Neanderthal for suggesting she might constitute a distraction on this mission. Nick could imagine her response if she knew the way his gut twisted every time he remembered how close those bullets had come to ripping into her.

"I'm still working out an operational strategy,"

he replied with perfect truth. His glance roamed the small restaurant. "But this isn't the time or the place to talk about it."

Mackenzie recognized a brush-off when she heard it. Her fingers drummed on the tablecloth for a moment or two.

Okay. If that's the way he wanted to play it, she'd go along. For now. But she intended to make it clear she considered herself a fully functioning member of this little team.

Which is why she exited her bedroom later that night and made her way across the sitting room toward his.

It was well past midnight Nice time, but still early by D.C. count. She'd heard Nick's shower cut off some time ago, had seen his lights go out. She'd turned off her lights, too, then tossed and turned on her regal bed for some time until finally deciding this was as good a time as any to have it out with him. If the time difference had kept her awake, she'd bet Nick wasn't asleep, either.

He wasn't, she discovered after rapping on his door a second time. Nor was he in his room.

The intrusion detection devices she'd set up were still activated, the silent alarms hadn't triggered, but Nick had vanished into the night.

Chapter 5

A silent shadow in black, Nick slipped through the darkened streets of Cannes. The moon had disappeared behind a bank of clouds. Light from the wrought iron streetlamps barely penetrated the gloom. Yet he wound his way unerringly through the twisting alleys.

These dark, crowded streets were home—the only home Henri Nicolas Everard had known until Maggie Sinclair and Paige Jensen had descended on Cannes all those years ago, followed in short order by their soon-to-be spouses. The OMEGA operatives had come to track down the reclusive megalomaniac responsible for pirating highly classified digital imaging technology. They'd left with a skinny, nimble-fingered pickpocket in tow.

After more than two decades in the States, Nick thought, felt, acted and spoke like an American, but the razor-edged survival instincts that had saved his life more than once during his years with OMEGA had been developed right here in Cannes. It was here he'd learned to blend with the darkness and become part of the night. Here he'd graduated from pocketknives to switchblades to razor-edged daggers. Here he'd slipped up like a shadow to relieve the rich and ultrarich of their wallets and watches.

Cannes was smaller than Nice, and more crowded. Its wealthy citizens occupied sumptuous villas dotting the hills above the city and ventured down only to visit the exclusive clubs, hotels and boutiques lining Cannes's fabled La Croisette. Few wandered into the heart of the old city, where Nick's destination lay—a small pawnshop a few blocks off the Place de la Castre. The owner was Jacques Gireaux, one of Nick's oldest and least reputable acquaintances.

If someone within a fifty-mile radius of Cannes had put Nick Jensen on a hit list, Gireaux would have heard about it. The man had a finger in or an eye on every shady operation on the Côte d'Azur. His small army of pickpockets brought him the rumors they picked up on the streets along with their haul of filched purses, rings and Rolexes. For years, Gireaux had fenced the goods Nick brought him... after taking his seventy-five percent commission, of course. As he'd frequently remind his minions, business was business.

Evidently business had fallen off considerably in recent years. Nick stood for some time in the shadows across the street from Gireaux's shop, noting its dust-streaked windows and upswept stoop. He saw no signs of activity, no light glowing from the back office or from the windows of the flat above the shop. Frowning, he crossed the street to read the small white sign affixed to the bars on the front door.

"Well, hell!"

It was an official notice, announcing a public auction. All items not claimed at these premises within sixty days would be sold to the highest bidder. He bent to peer at the date and caught a glimpse of a red glow in the entry to the shop next door.

His muscles coiled. With a flick of his right wrist, the handle of a knife slid into his palm. Turning, he searched the shadows.

"The shop is closed, monsieur."

A small, slight figure emerged from the darkened entry. He looked to be about eight or nine, but the cigarette dangling from his lip and the way he

moved told Nick the kid didn't count his age in
years.

With a jerk of his chin, the boy indicated the
barred door. "This shop is closed," he said again.
"I can take you to another, where you will get good
prices for whatever it is you wish to sell."

"My business is with Gireaux. Where is he?"

The kid ran a considering eye over Nick's length.
The dark clothes gave him pause, but not enough
to keep him from conducting a little business of his
own.

"Such information should be worth a few francs,
yes?"

"How many francs?"

The cigarette's tip glowed bright red-gold.

"Fifty."

Nick knew the rules. He'd played this game often
enough himself. The kid expected him to bargain
the price of his information down to twenty, maybe
ten francs. Digging into his pocket, Nick extracted
his wallet and produced a hundred franc note.

The diminutive informant didn't hesitate. With a
flash of his small, nimble fingers he plucked the
note out of Nick's hand. It disappeared inside the
pockets to his grubby shorts.

"I regret, monsieur, I have no change."

"Somehow I didn't think you would. So where's
Gireaux?"

"He is dead."

"Dead how?"

"He was shot, right there in his shop, two... No, three weeks ago."

The timing could be coincidence. Mere chance. Nick wouldn't bet on it.

"How did it happen?"

"Thieves broke in hoping to find Gireaux's cash box. They found him instead. There was some unpleasantness, you understand, before they put a bullet through his head and ended his misery."

"What kind of unpleasantness?"

"Fingernails pulled off," the boy said with a shrug that indicated little sympathy for the deceased. "An electric wire up his nose. Me, I think they fried his brains and had no choice but to shoot him. All they made off with were some papers."

Interesting. Nick knew Gireaux cooked his books. He'd had to in order to survive regular visits from gendarmes searching for stolen property. To keep himself straight, however, he maintained a secret set of records. Nick had seen him hunched over the ledger, scribbling down who had brought in what, along with the estimated value of the items. Those records, the pawnbroker would chuckle, the police would never find.

Maybe the thieves hadn't found them, either.

With a nod to the kid, Nick spun on one heel and

walked away. Ten minutes and six backtracking
turns later, he inserted one of Mackenzie's handy-
dandy electronic gadgets into the shop's rear door.
The wafer-thin device used a kind of sonar to
bounce silent signals off the tumblers in a lock, then
sized a set of teeth to open them.

Good thing Mackenzie hadn't decided on a life
of crime, Nick thought with a grim smile as the lock
clicked open. There wasn't a security system or a
bank safe she couldn't get around. With Nick's own
talents in that arena, they would have made an un-
stoppable team in the old days.

Putting the thought from his mind, he closed the
door behind him and switched on a pencil-thin
beam of light. He needed the light to navigate the
clutter of items pawned long ago for a fraction of
their value and never reclaimed. A cello leaned
drunkenly against a mannequin draped in moth-
eaten mink. Bicycles, lawn chairs and chain saws
dangled from ceiling hooks. An antique Louis XV
glass-fronted cabinet displayed a collection of cos-
tume jewelry and cameras. The really high-value
items—the diamond tennis bracelets, the dinner
rings, the high-priced watches—would be in the
safe hidden under the floorboards in Gireaux's upstairs office.

The pawnshop owner never knew that one of his
street rats had shimmied up a drainpipe one night.

After crawling through a window, the toothpick-thin pickpocket had watched Gireaux pry up the floorboards to deposit the 60" string of lustrous matched pearls Nick lifted earlier that afternoon. He'd never mentioned what he saw that night to anyone, Gireaux in particular. Rumor was the cold-blooded shop owner had strangled one particularly troublesome street punk with his own hands and dumped the body in the bay. Nick had possessed no desire to feed the sharks.

The safe was right where he remembered it, hidden beneath floorboards so dusty they looked as though they hadn't been swept since the previous century. Nick slid the tip of his blade between the boards until he located the spring that released them. Another of Mackenzie's supersensitive devices delivered the necessary amplification to hear the click of the spin lock as it disengaged. Thoughtfully, Nick surveyed the velvet drawstring bags nestled inside.

Was this what the thieves had been after? This hidden stash?

His gloved fingers slipped the knot on one bag and a waterfall of sparkling emeralds slid into his palm. The stones were grouped in star shaped patterns to form a three-inch wide choker.

Nick recognized the necklace instantly. It had last graced the neck of one of America's most volup-

tuous film stars. A jeweler anxious for free publicity
had pressed her to wear the heavily insured choker
at the Cannes film festival some years ago.

The necklace had disappeared the second night
of the festival, and the attendant hue and cry had
generated plenty of publicity, if not the kind the
jeweler had anticipated. No wonder Gireaux had
kept the piece hidden away. He'd been waiting for
the heat to die down before trying to find a private
buyer.

Nick played with the sparkling gems, remembering how they'd gleamed above the movie star's
overripe breasts. They deserved a more elegant setting, a less overwhelming platform. A smile tugged
at his mouth as he imagined them around Mackenzie's throat. With her green cat's eyes and creamy
skin, she'd look magnificent stretched out on a silk
coverlet wearing these emeralds.

Only these emeralds.

The smile slipped. His body went taut. He could
see her sprawled on the fluffy duvet. Feel her under
him. Her long legs tangled with his, her mouth open
and eager. Sweating under his black turtleneck, he
slid the glittering stones back into their bag.

Gireaux's ledgers lay at the bottom of the safe.
Nick flipped through the later ones, not surprised
at the shop owner's meticulous attention to detail.

Or by the names and addresses annotated in the margins.

For years Gireaux had made a double killing by blackmailing clients who'd lost wallets or purses containing compromising bits of information. Love notes from mistresses. Phone numbers for male prostitutes. Notices from the bank about late payments or overdue accounts. Gireaux had also sold stolen passports, IDs and credit cards on the black market. Both sidelines were dangerous. One might finally have gotten the old man killed.

The ledgers containing Henri Nicolas Everard's contributions to these shady enterprises spanned some six years. Shaking his head, Nick skimmed a glance down the handwritten entries. He knew he'd been quick and at times incredibly bold, but he hadn't realized he'd raked in such a haul.

Despite the incriminating evidence, he hadn't come to destroy the ledgers. The statute of limitations on his crimes had run out years ago. Nor was Nick particularly worried about having his past exposed. He wielded enough influence—and wealth—to put his own spin on whatever story might come out. Besides, his gut told him these books held the key to the murderous attacks on both him and on Gireaux.

Stuffing the ledgers into the black cloth sack he'd brought with him for just this purpose, he piled the velvet sacks back in the safe. All except the one containing the emeralds.

He'd have to come up with a credible story for how the collar came into his possession. Reimburse the insurance company for any payments to the jeweler who'd loaned out the necklace. Convince Mackenzie to wear them.

Grinning, he slipped the bag into his pocket.

It was close to dawn by the time he'd made the drive back to Nice. Leaving the rental car in the hotel's garage, he avoided the lobby and slipped up the back stairs. A quick flick with a small, handheld device directed a high-energy beam at the camera hidden in a vent. The beam temporarily blinded its electronic eye. For the few moments it took Nick to reach their suite, the lens would record nothing but gray fuzz.

The same device deactivated the intrusion detection devices Mackenzie had set up inside their suite. Two clicks, and Nick could use the key card without fear of setting off the silent alarms.

The sitting room was dark, the air saturated with the perfume of gladiolas. Nick entered on silent, rubber-soled shoes and speared a quick glance at the bedroom opposite his. Not so much as a glimmer of light showed under Mackenzie's closed door. He started for his own room, took only two steps, and felt a small prod at his left shoulder.

Pain jolted into him. Sharp. Slicing. His muscles contracted with shock. He lurched forward, but couldn't coordinate his movements.

Swearing viciously, he went down.

Chapter 6

Nick's right knee hit the carpet. He managed to keep from toppling over. Barely. Whoever had zapped him had used just enough juice to get his attention. The pain in his shoulder was ferocious, but not unbearable. From past experience, he knew he'd regain control over his muscles shortly.

When he did...

With savage intensity, he fought the pain. Suddenly, the lights flicked on and flooded the suite with a golden glow.

"Well, well," a voice drawled from just behind him. "Look who the cat dragged in."

Silk swished. A figure draped in pale silver

moved into the periphery of Nick's vision. With an effort that caused beads of sweat to pop out on his temples, he raised his head.

With casual unconcern for the voltage she'd just drilled into him, Mackenzie tossed a pencil-thin Taser onto a nearby table. Her glance was decidedly unsympathetic as it swept over his hunched form.

"You really shouldn't sneak into hotel rooms in the middle of the night, Nick. Or disable the silent alarms. I thought you were one of the bad guys breaking in."

The hell she had! She'd known exactly who she'd taken down. The look he shot her could have peeled the bark from a tree, but Mackenzie didn't so much as blink.

"For that matter," she continued, nonchalantly crossing her arms, "you really shouldn't sneak *out* of hotel rooms in the middle of the night. What was I supposed to think when I went to your room and found you gone?"

He could tell from the tight set to her jaw that she was royally torqued. Nick wasn't feeling too friendly at the moment, either. He didn't know which got to him more. The fact that she'd taken him down so easily or that she'd obviously decided to teach him a lesson.

Maybe it was time to teach Ms. Blair a thing or two.

Still propped on one knee, he grunted and reached for the strap of the cloth bag slung over his shoulder. He kept his movements slow, awkward… until his fingers wrapped around the strap. Without any warning, his arm whipped forward and brought the heavy ledgers in an arc that knocked Mackenzie's feet out from under her.

"Hey!"

Nick lunged and caught her as she tumbled down. He managed to keep her tailbone from thumping the floor, then used her momentum to carry them both backward. His body landed on hers. Using its weight to keep her down, he grabbed her flailing arms and pinned them to the carpet. She bucked once or twice, more from surprise than from any real hope of dislodging him.

Deliberately, Nick relaxed his taut muscles and let her take his full weight. The air whooshed out of her lungs, and the fire went out of her eyes.

"Nick! I can't…breathe."

He eased his weight up on his elbows, but kept her under him. She pulled air back in with breathy little pants.

"All right," she gasped. "That's one takedown apiece. We're even."

"Not quite."

The low growl made Mackenzie blink. She took in the skin stretched tight across his cheeks, the narrowed eyes, the clenched jaw. This was Lightning, the lethal operative she'd glimpsed in action the night of the attack. The same operative who'd sent a kitchen knife across a room with blinding speed.

Belatedly, it occurred to her that she might have unleashed something she could have trouble controlling. Wariness fluttered in her veins, overlaying the anger that had simmered there since she'd discovered him gone.

"Nick…"

Ignoring her breathless gasp, he stretched her arms high above her head and transferred both wrists into one hand. When he brought his free arm down and slid it beneath the small of her back, Mackenzie's pulse skittered. Stopped. Started again with a painful kick.

"Don't even think about it," she panted, reading his intent in his face.

"Too late."

His mouth came down on hers, and a dozen different responses flashed into Mackenzie's head. She could jerk up her knee. Crack her forehead against his. Sink her teeth into the lips savaging hers.

But this was Nick. The man she worked with and for. Despite the aura of danger that crackled around him like summer lightning, he'd back off if she put up a fight. She was almost sure of it.

By the time her conscious mind had reasoned that

out, the pleasure centers in her brain had begun shooting out traitorous little synapses. The urge to relax her lips, to open her mouth under his, jumped from nerve to nerve like a live spark.

Nick, damn him, played to her body, not her mind. As if sensing the electricity racing through her, he slanted his mouth over hers. The hold on her wrists loosened. The arm curved around her waist tightened.

They were molded together, hip to hip, chest to chest. Her breasts were mashed flat. Her pelvis rocked against his. Through the thin silk of her nightgown, Mackenzie felt him harden and press against her stomach. The muscles low in her belly spasmed in instinctive response even as alarms clanged like crazy in her head.

Whoa! Time to end things, right here, right now. While she still could.

To her profound annoyance, Nick beat her to the draw. Breaking off the kiss, he raised his head and frowned down at her. Listening to his breath rasp out as fast and rough as hers gave Mackenzie a perverse and very intense satisfaction. Smooth, sure, in-control Nick Jensen had come as close to losing it as she had.

"Are we even now?" she asked pointedly.

"We're getting there."

"Then how about you let me up?"

The crease between his sun-bleached brows disappeared. Right before her eyes, the Nick she knew reemerged. Seemingly more amused than annoyed.

"Am I going to have to fight you for the Taser when I do?"

"We'll decide that when I'm on my feet."

With a nod, he disengaged. If he felt any lingering discomfort—above or below his belt—it didn't show in his lithe movements. When he reached down a hand to help her up, Mackenzie decided it would be undignified at this point to swat it away. Scrambling to her feet, she twitched her pale silver gown into place.

"Okay, Nick, the fun and games are over. Where did you go tonight?"

"To Cannes, to visit an old business associate."

"And you didn't tell me because?"

"One, I wasn't sure the trip would produce anything significant. Two…"

"Yes?"

He raked a hand through the tawny gold of his hair. "Two, I wasn't ready to explain how I knew this particular associate."

Curiosity spiked into Mackenzie, layering on top of the chaotic sensations the man had already roused. Evidently she was about to learn something about Lightning's past.

"Why don't you call room service and order up

a pot of coffee while I get changed?'' she suggested. ''This doesn't sound like the kind of conversation we should conduct while one of us is
wearing a nightgown.''

''Not that nightgown,'' Nick agreed, his voice
laced with genuine regret.

The moment she closed her bedroom door, Mackenzie collapsed against it.

For all her seemingly quick recovery out there in
the sitting room, she needed time to get her runaway pulse back under control. Not to mention
douse the fire still raging throughout her body.

In retrospect she had to admit zapping Nick with
the Taser hadn't been such a good idea. She'd intended to make a very succinct, very dramatic point.
She'd accomplished that.

So had he.

Gulping, she drew her tongue along her lower lip.
She could still taste him. Still feel him. Not just on
her lips. Her breasts tingled from their contact with
his chest, and the tight little ache low in her belly
refused to go away. All she had to do was remember Nick rock-hard against her and the ache intensified to a hot, pulsing need.

Dammit! She'd known she wasn't in Nick Jensen's league, but she hadn't realized just how far
out of it she was. One taste of his mouth on hers,

one press of his hips against her thighs, and she'd almost forgotten the hard-learned lessons from her marriage.

She should have been the one to break off the kiss. She should have dredged up a superior smile and that thoroughly annoying glint of amusement. She should have rolled to her feet and helped him up instead of lying in a puddle of want at his feet.

That wouldn't happen again! If and when she and Nick tangled again, she'd make sure she came out on top.

Groaning at the erotic and wholly inappropriate image that flashed into her head, Mackenzie shoved away from the door and marched to the massive armoire where she'd hung her new wardrobe. After a quick review of the selections, she pulled on a pair of tan linen slacks and a cropped navy blue sweater with a nautical design in white and gold.

Three hours, two pots of coffee and six scanned ledgers later, Mackenzie reviewed the list she'd compiled on her laptop computer. Her lips rounding in a soundless whistle, she turned to the man sprawled comfortably on the elegant Empire sofa.

"You really stole all this stuff?"

"That and more. Gireaux only annotated the items he considered high-value in his secret set of books. There's no telling how many Timexes, Kodak Instamatics and fake tennis bracelets I lifted that didn't warrant an entry in the ledgers.''

Nick Jensen, a thief. Mackenzie was having trouble making the mental adjustment.

''How long were you on the streets?'' she asked curiously.

''I'm not sure. I must have been about four or five when Gireaux caught me filching fruit from a market stall and took me under his wing. I'd been living on what I could steal for some time before that.''

''What happened to your parents?''

His shoulders lifted in a careless shrug. ''I don't have any idea who my father was. Neither, I'm told, did my mother. She sold herself to buy cocaine and OD'ed when she was eighteen or nineteen.''

''Good Lord!''

''Feeling sorry for me?'' he asked with a smile. ''Don't. Paige and Doc Jensen were the best parents any kid could ever hope for. They more than made up for the holes in my early years—not that I felt particularly deprived at the time.'' His smile widened. ''I was an enterprising little runt. As you can see from that list, I usually took in a pretty good haul.''

With some effort, Mackenzie wrenched her mind away from this fascinating glimpse into Nick's past.

"Do you really think there's a connection between the attack in D.C. and this Jacques Gireaux?"

"I'd say the interval between his murder and the attack on us was too close to be mere coincidence. My bet is that whoever broke into his shop found something that linked him to me. I just haven't established what that link is yet."

"I guess this list is as good a place to start looking as any," Mackenzie murmured, scrolling down the entries she'd transferred from the ledgers to her laptop. "The jewelry and watches are no problem. I can bounce them against the International Jewelers' Database and retrieve information on items by ID number, purchase date, owner or vendor. If I cross-check that with various insurance claims databases, we can see who filed claims on which pieces. Ditto the cameras and the laptop. But this stuff…"

She highlighted several items with the pointer.

"Two sets, deep-sea fishing rods and reels. One each, ladies beaded evening bag, butterfly shape. A porcelain *bourdalou,* circa 1815. What the heck is that?"

"A portable chamber pot. Designed for ladies' relief during particularly tedious church sessions, when they were locked into their pews. The vessels also came in handy on long journeys. In England, I believe they were called coach pots."

"A porta-potty, huh? I don't even want to guess where you swiped that from."

Nick flashed her a grin. "An antique shop. I'd followed a pair of plump pigeons inside, but the shop owner took after me before I could relieve his customers of their wallets. Not one to leave empty-handed, I snatched the *bourdalou* as I exited the premises. It turned out to be one of my best takes."

Mackenzie checked the amount Gireaux had received for the stolen antique and whistled. "I guess so!"

Nick's grin took on a rueful slant. He'd returned to the antique shop decades later and purchased a set of twenty-four karat gold-rimmed china that had once graced the table of Louis XV. Although Nick had made a show of dickering, he paid twice what the completed set was worth, more than reimbursing the shop owner for the loss of the chamber pot. The exquisite china was now showcased in his Paris restaurant and, ironically, had led to an invitation for Monsieur Jensen to become a patron of the International Porcelain Collectors' Society.

Nick had engineered similar ruses over the years to repay the cost of other items he'd stolen, but none had taken quite as big a chunk out of his wallet. Now that he had a complete list of his transactions with Gireaux, though, he'd no doubt soon start shelling out more disguised reimbursements.

Assuming, that is, Mackenzie worked her particular brand of magic and put the names of owners to all or most of the items.

She was already hard at it. She had one leg tucked under her. Her third cup of coffee sat close at hand as her fingers flew over the keys of her laptop. She'd clipped her dark hair up, out of the way, and stuck a pen through its dark mass. She appeared cool and calm and thoroughly competent, but all Nick could see was a flushed, furious Mackenzie sprawled beneath him on the carpet.

He still couldn't quite believe she'd used that damned cattle prod on him. Or that he'd had to battle a savage urge to take what she wasn't ready to give. For a few moments, with Mackenzie's body pinned under his, his layers of civilization had peeled away. He'd wanted to do more than just subdue her. He'd wanted to claim her.

Even now, just sitting here watching her scowl at the computer screen evoked primitive impulses that were more suited to a cave than an elegantly furnished suite in one of the world's most expensive hotels.

He had it bad, Nick thought, blowing out a breath. Much worse than he'd realized. And now that he'd shown Mackenzie a glimpse of what lurked beneath his veneer of sophistication, he suspected he'd have a tough time regaining lost ground…both as her boss and the man who was determined to finish what they'd started a little while ago on the floor.

This, Nick thought wryly, was going to take every ounce of finesse he possessed and then some. Uncoiling his long length, he abandoned the sofa.

"You do your magic," he said when Mackenzie glanced up with a question in her eyes. "I'll shower and change, then take you to the Cours Saleya."

"Which is?"

"The heart of the city. Sooner or later you'll run into every Niçois there."

Nodding, Mackenzie went back to clicking the keys. Her fingers stilled when Nick entered his bedroom, however. She sat, chewing her lower lip, until she picked up the faint drum of his shower.

The session with the Taser had made her cautious. Very cautious. But she had no intention of being left behind to stew the next time Nick decided to take off on his own.

Easing out of her chair, she went to her own room and dug into her bag of tricks. A moment later, she extracted a small, flat disc that contained the latest in homing devices. The composite material encasing the hair-thin transmitter was as supple as Saran Wrap and allowed for much higher conductivity. The signal this baby sent out consisted of short, variable pulses that defied interception and interpretation by anyone who didn't have access to the code. Unless OMEGA had been completely compromised, Mackenzie was the only person in the south of France who possessed that code.

Her heart hammering, she slipped into Nick's room. Steam rolled from the open door to the bath. With an ear tuned to the pulsing shower, she moved to the antique dresser. Her breath eased out in a sigh of relief when she spotted his watch among a scatter of keys and loose change.

In less than a minute, she'd pried off the watch's back, stuck the transmitter to the inside and snapped the case shut.

She was back at her computer, keys clicking, when Nick emerged from his bedroom. The black slacks and turtleneck were gone. So was the gold stubble that had shaded his cheeks and chin. In charcoal-gray slacks, Italian leather shoes and belt, and a white linen shirt with the neck open and the sleeves rolled up, he didn't look like a cat burglar who'd broken into a Cannes pawnshop in the middle of the night. Nor like the furious, tight-jawed agent who'd knocked Mackenzie's feet out from under her and tumbled her to the floor. With a dart of satisfaction, she saw he was wearing his watch.

"Ready to take a break?" he asked.

"I might as well. I've cross-referenced all the

items by type and date stolen and fired off inquiries
to every database OMEGA has legal access to.''

And a few they didn't. She'd disguised the inquiries to make sure the cyber police couldn't track
them back to either her or OMEGA. In the remote
chance they did, she figured getting shot at by thugs
gave her certain extraordinary privileges.

''This would have been easier and quicker if you
hadn't been such a prolific thief,'' she commented,
flipping down the lid of the laptop.

''Everyone should be good at something.''

She could name a few other things this man was
good at. Her mouth still tingled from the force of
his kiss. So did the sensitive tips of her breasts.

''When do you think we'll start getting replies to
your queries?''

''Hopefully, we'll have some waiting for us
when we get back,'' she replied as he escorted her
out of the suite. ''Where are we going, again?''

''The Cours Saleya. Nice's open-air market.''

Chapter 7

The limo driver's tale of the obese laundress had tickled Mackenzie's sense of humor and engendered a certain level of affection for Nice. The Cours Saleya tumbled her right into love with the city.

Her years in the military had taken her to dozens of foreign countries and countless open-air markets. Many were larger than this one. Some were more elaborate. But none assaulted her senses with such a brilliant profusion of color and scents. The flowers and fruits alone were enough to make her wish she'd graduated beyond paint-by-the-numbers.

Gloriously purple irises, bloodred gladiolas, kiss-me-pink geraniums and endless banks of sunshine-yellow mums dazzled and delighted her eye. The fruit stalls were just as vivid, with tall pyramids of pomegranates, artful displays of grapes and kaleidoscopes of kiwi, oranges, lemons and limes.

Cases of marzipan sat side by side with the real thing. The candy strawberries, apples, pears and cherries were so skillfully crafted and displayed that at first glance Mackenzie didn't realize they weren't the authentic items.

But it was the spice market that stole her heart. Her nostrils tingling, she drank in the pungent tang of wild onions and garlic. Rosemary, thyme and sage. Lavender. Dill. Marjoram. Dozens of other exotic aromas she couldn't identify. While her olfactory nerves tried to sort them all out, her delighted gaze roamed the displays under the tented awnings.

The wild explosion of color must have sent Matisse and Picasso into raptures. Although the spices themselves were dried and mostly grayish-green in color, the wily merchants presented them in small, square baskets lined with a variety of brightly colored cloth napkins. The lavender-blues and sunshine-yellows that seemed to characterize the south of France predominated, accented by splashes of red and green and poppy-pink.

"I've never seen anything like this," Mackenzie

murmured to Nick. "Nature used every color in her palette to paint this scene."

"Nature and the Niçois," he answered with a smile.

His glance roamed the scene, taking in the rows of tented stalls, the housewives with long, crusty baguettes poking from their shopping bags, the tourists bused over from the cruise ships docked at nearby Monaco.

Nick never felt at home, really at home, until he hit the morning market and drank in the aroma of the spices that grew so plentifully in the hills above the Côte d'Azur. Of course, the thronged aisles between the stalls might have something to do with his sense of coming home. He'd lifted many a camera and wallet in crowded marketplaces just like this one.

The suspicion that his years of thievery were now coming back to haunt him was fast hardening into certainty. The phone call he'd made to the Cannes Inspector of Police this morning had forged another link in the chain. He waited until he and Mackenzie claimed a table at one of the sidewalk cafés that ringed the market to tell her about the call.

"I talked to the Inspector of Police in Cannes this morning," he said over coffee and croissants still warm from the oven.

"You did? When?"

"After I got out of the shower."

"Why didn't you tell me?"

"I am telling you."

Her brows snapped together. "It would be nice if you clued me in about little things like breaking into pawnshops and conversations with the police before you decide to have them, not after the fact."

The retort won her a sharp look from OMEGA's director. "Careful, Comm."

With exaggerated care, Mackenzie placed her knife and flaky croissant on her plate. "Pulling rank on me, Lightning?"

"If I have to."

"Don't you think it's a little late for that?"

She was right. They'd crossed the line between boss and subordinate this morning, Mackenzie by deliberately poking that damned cattle prod into his shoulder, Nick by stretching her out under him and taking the taste he'd been craving for months now. They both knew they couldn't step back over that line, but where the hell they went from here was still up for discussion. With a nod, Nick accepted full responsibility for their altered and as yet undefined relationship.

"You're right. I let matters get out of hand this morning. I apologize."

The apology took Mackenzie by surprise... almost as much as the promise that followed.

"It won't happen again."

Well, hell! He beat her to the punch again! *She* had intended to make that calm pronouncement, just as *she* had intended to break off the kiss earlier this morning. It was tough trying to claim the high moral ground when the man kept cutting it out from under her.

Maybe it was time to stop trying. Nick had to have sensed the surge in her pulse this morning. Had to have guessed how that kiss affected her. Rather than deny the attraction, maybe she needed to be honest about why things couldn't go any further.

"Look, I admit there's a certain spark between us. We talked about it back in Washington. We also talked about the hazards of office affairs. They get too complicated, too messy."

"They can," he agreed, "if the parties involved allow it to happen." He lounged back in his chair, his gaze thoughtful. "But that's not the reason you're so determined to snuff out the spark, is it? Not the whole reason, anyway."

She glanced at the flower-filled stalls, remembering the fever, the excitement, the heady rush of tumbling into what she thought was love. Remembering, too, that she'd missed the mark by several nautical miles.

"Let's just say I've had my fingers burned and I'm not ready to play with fire again."

She thought he might nod solemnly. Offer sympathy for her bruised ego, if not her failed marriage. She certainly didn't expect a quick, slashing grin.

"Fair enough. When you *are* ready, just strike a match."

Mackenzie plopped back in her chair, more than a little suspicious of the power he'd just handed her. Nick Jensen, ready to snap to attention and spring into action when...if...she said the word. Why was she having trouble with this scenario?

Still, he wasn't the kind of man to renege on a promise. If he said the next move was up to her, it was up to her. That should certainly keep her tossing and turning for the next few nights. Or weeks.

Okay, years.

"Let's get back to the phone call you made this morning. Did the Cannes Inspector of Police have any interesting information to share about Jacques Gireaux's murder?"

"As a matter of fact, he did. The bullet they dug out of Gireaux's skull was fired from a .9mm Beretta."

Mackenzie sucked in a sharp breath. One of the thugs who attacked her and Nick had jerked a Beretta from an underarm holster just before she snatched up his Uzi and put him permanently out of commission.

"The Beretta is the standard-issue sidearm for half the armies and police forces in the world," she said, frowning. "It could be nothing more than coincidence that one of our uninvited visitors carried the same type weapon."

"It could, if you believe in coincidence. I asked the inspector to fax the ballistics report to the D.C. police. Be interesting to see if the rifling patterns on the spent shell casings match."

"Very."

"Would you like more coffee?"

She glanced down at her barely touched cup. "No, thanks. The two pots we downed earlier maxed out my caffeine meter for the day."

"Then we'd better get back to the hotel."

"Why?"

"There's someone I want to see."

A quick snap of his fingers brought the waiter to the table. Mackenzie waited until Nick had glanced at the tab and handed the man several franc notes.

"Is this someone you want to see another old associate?" she asked, ready to bristle if Nick intended to conduct his own private inquiries and leave her twiddling her thumbs again.

"Actually, it's the Negresco's owner. He's anx-

ious to continue our discussion about the possibility
of opening one of my restaurants at his hotel. Don't
worry, Comm,'' he added with a crooked grin.
''You made your point earlier. No more secrets between us…at least as far as this operation is con-
cerned. Agreed?''

''Agreed.''

Shooting a glance at his watch, he pushed back
his chair. ''Ready?''

Mackenzie hesitated, suddenly reminded of the
tracking device she'd planted on him. No sense upsetting the fragile truce she and Nick had just hammered out, she decided. She'd remove it later.

That was her intent, anyway. Time and circum-
stance conspired against her.

They returned to the hotel to find the message
light on the phone flashing and a ton of e-mails
piled up on Mackenzie's laptop. While Nick re-
trieved his phone messages, she tossed her purse
onto a chair and skimmed the list of messages.

''They're mostly answers to the queries I zinged
off earlier,'' she related when he finished with the
phone and crossed the room to peer over her shoulder.

''What about updates from the control center?
Did Ace send in a status report?''

''Yep. Right here.''

Mackenzie displayed the message, which contained little more than a brief confirmation that the OMEGA operative was still in covert mode, slogging it out in the Saudi oil fields. The crew manning the control center would have contacted her or Nick immediately if Ace had run into trouble. Or stumbled on any real leads as to who was behind the sabotage of several major refineries some months ago.

"Tell your people to patch Ace through to me the next time he reports in," Nick instructed. "I want to hear how it's going."

Lightning was back in director mode. Although the chain of command had blurred considerably during those moments he and Mackenzie had spent on the floor, she understood the weight of the responsibilities he carried.

"Will do."

With a click of a few keys, she transmitted the order and swiveled around in her chair. "Ace has been in place for over a month now. When are we going to bring him home?"

"When we can assure the president those oil field explosions weren't engineered by one of the radical, anti-Arab hate groups that sprang up in the States after 9-11."

The terse reply underscored the potential diplomatic minefield that had prompted the presidential

decision to send in an OMEGA agent. As if the
suicide bomb attacks in Israel, Iraq's stubborn re-
fusal to grant access by U.N. inspectors and esca-
lating anti-U.S. sentiment over the war in Afghan-
istan hadn't poured enough fuel on the fire. Now,
person or persons unknown were attempting to dis-
rupt the petro-economy of the U.S.'s strongest ally
among the Pan-Arab states. If it should turn out that
American hate groups had funded or otherwise supported the sabotage, the situation in the Middle East
could very well go from bad to catastrophic.

With a distinct sympathy for the pressure piling
up on Ace's shoulders, she turned her thoughts to
the situation she and Nick now found themselves
in. She was anxious to start bouncing the replies to
her queries off the list she and Nick had compiled
earlier, but equally as curious about the phone messages he'd received.

He didn't keep her in suspense. As he'd anticipated, word of Nick Jensen's arrival had already
circulated. So had the fact that he'd brought along
an "associate."

"We're invited for cocktails with Tom Cruise
later this afternoon. He and Penelope are spending
the week at a villa in St. Tropez."

"Well, what do you know! And here I was thinking there was only limited upside to almost having

my body pierced in several dozen places by a couple of thugs.''

Nick allowed Mackenzie all of two seconds to enjoy the glorious fantasy of drinks with Tom and Penelope on a sun-washed balcony overlooking the sea.

''Unfortunately, we'll have to make it another time. Countess d'Ariancourt also issued an invitation. She's having a small soiree at her home tonight, only forty or so guests. She'd be delighted if we could attend.''

Mackenzie groaned in disappointment. ''Who's Countess d'Ariancourt?''

''Something of a legend along the Riviera.'' A smile played at the corners of Nick's mouth. ''Sooner or later, everyone with any wealth or influence finds their way to her salon.''

With profound regrets to Tom and Penelope, Mackenzie bowed to the inevitable. ''You'd better give me some pointers. What does one wear to a small soiree of forty or so?''

''Pull out all the stops. Dianthe certainly will.''

Dianthe, was it?

Interesting.

Nick's meeting with the Negresco's owner spilled over into the afternoon. Mackenzie spent the hours sorting through the replies to her e-mails and shooting off a new series of queries. By late afternoon, she'd identified the owners of a good number of the items Nick had pilfered during his years on the streets. It helped that he'd developed a sharp eye early in his career as a thief and had only gone for the good stuff. Most of the owners had been compensated for their losses. A few, she noted, had later reported the missing items returned.

She zinged those names to her folks at OMEGA's control center, with instructions to contact them for details about the return of their property. She also requested they bounce the owners off law enforcement and intelligence databases, looking for possible links to illegal activities or terrorist groups.

That done, she skimmed the list of items that hadn't returned any information. The fishing reels fell into that category, as did several less expensive cameras, the butterfly-shaped evening bag, a cane with a handle of embossed silver and a set of dentures carved from solid ivory.

Shaking her head over the last item, Mackenzie played on the Internet for the rest of the afternoon, running searches for any items similar to those on the list. She was more than ready to quit when Nick returned from his meeting and suggested a light dinner on the balcony.

Then it was time to go through her new wardrobe. Draping several outfits across the bed, Mackenzie debated the selections. First, she tried on a strapless sheath of flame-colored silk. Slit high on one side, it was elegant, yet not ostentatious. But when she slipped into wide-legged white chiffon palazzo pants and a matching bustier encrusted with shimmering Swarovski crystals, she knew she had a winner.

Oh, yes! This was it!

The seductive little top left her neck and shoulders bare. The chiffon pants flowed around her like a cloud, seemingly demure until she moved and displayed the silhouette of her legs. Sweeping up her newly trimmed hair, she anchored the dark mass with a comb twinkling with the same sparkling crystals. Strappy silver sandals and a sequined evening bag completed the ensemble.

Twirling this way and that, Mackenzie admired the new, improved her in the mirror. Too bad Tom Baby couldn't see her in this little number.

Nick's reaction almost made up for the disappointment of missing out on Cruise and Cruz. He was standing next to the marble fireplace. With one hand in the pocket of his tux jacket and one wrapped loosely around the stem of a Baccarat champagne goblet, he epitomized masculine elegance and wealth. No one observing him at this moment—Mackenzie included—would ever have imagined that he once had to steal to eat.

Gliding into the room, she executed a slow twirl. The chiffon pants flared in a wide circle. "Well? Do I pass muster?"

Nick's eyes drifted from her throat to her toes and back again. The admiration in their blue depths sent a ripple of feminine satisfaction down Mackenzie's spine. Instead of the compliment she fully expected, though, he cocked his head and made another survey.

"You look spectacular, but the outfit needs..."

"What?"

"A touch of color. Emeralds I think, to match your eyes."

"Riiiight. Too bad Field Dress Unit's budget only runs to crystals, not emeralds."

"Luckily I have my own resources to draw on."

Calmly, he placed his champagne goblet on the mantle, trading it for a black velvet bag. Unknotting the gold strings, he spilled a river of sparkling green into his palms.

"Good Lord!" Mackenzie gasped. "Where did you get this?"

"From Gireaux's safe."

"Nick! Is it stolen property?"

"Most likely."

"I can't wear it in public! Someone might recognize the piece."

"I'm hoping someone does." Unperturbed, he moved behind her and draped the collar around her throat. "It's time to stir things up a bit."

"Well, this should certainly do it," she retorted, checking out the necklace in the mirror above the mantel.

Chapter 8

The Negresco's friendly limo driver chauffeured them to Countess d'Ariancourt's villa. The trip took some time, as the narrow road leading up to the elegant residences in the hills above the city snaked back and forth in dizzying, one-hundred-eighty-degree curves. Jean-Claude took the limo through the hairpin turns like a trainer putting a thoroughbred through its paces.

Finally, he pulled into a cobbled court crowded with Rolls-Royces and Bentleys and handed Mackenzie out. Breathing deeply, she drank in the heady perfume and spectacular colors of the evening. Bougainvillea spilled over the courtyard's walls in glorious shades of red and pink. Below what looked like a sheer, thousand-foot drop, lacy white waves curled on a sea just deepening to cobalt.

If the view stole Mackenzie's breath, the villa completely enchanted her. With its gray slate mansards and fanciful stonework above the doors and windows, it was a magnificently restored relic of a more opulent era.

So, she soon discovered, was its owner.

A stately majordomo escorted the new arrivals to the villa's second floor salon, which ran the entire length of the house. Chandeliers dripping with crystal showered light on exquisitely frescoed walls. Circular settees tufted in shimmering gold velvet were spaced at intervals down the middle of the room to allow the guests to sit or circulate with ease. Potted palms added an airy touch of green to the belle epoch opulence.

When the majordomo announced them, their hostess separated from the glittering, bejeweled crowd.

''Nicolas!''

Gliding across the salon, the petite, raven-haired aristocrat thrust out hands weighted down with more rocks than the coast of Maine.

''Darling, darling Nicolas!''

''Hello, Dianthe.''

Smiling, she lifted her face to Nick's. No polite pecks on the cheek for the countess, Mackenzie noted. She took his kiss full on her mouth. When Nick raised his head, her smile worked into a kittenish pout that should have looked ridiculous on a woman her age.

Should being the operative word, Mackenzie acknowledged wryly. The woman had to be a good twenty years older than Nick, yet exuded a stunning, sensual vitality that made time seem irrelevant…along with every other female in the room.

"It's been so long, Nicolas. Too long."

"Yes, it has."

"But now you've come back to me." She tucked her arm in his. "You'll stay in Nice for the opening of opera season, won't you? You quite spoiled me the last time you were here, you wretch. I can't bear to listen to Mahler any more without you murmuring your droll commentary in my ear."

"Our plans are uncertain as yet."

"Our? Oh, yes. I was told you brought your…" Her violet eyes flicked to Mackenzie, lingered on the emeralds, took on a gleam of amused comprehension. "Your associate, is it not?"

With a private, I-told-you-so grin, Nick made the introductions.

"May I present Ms. Mackenzie Blair, CEO of Blair Communications?" he said smoothly, using the cover Mackenzie had developed years ago to disguise her work for OMEGA. "She's an expert in her field, and one of my most capable partners."

The countess slid another look at the emeralds and gave a throaty gurgle of laughter.

"Obviously."

Okay. Enough was enough. Mackenzie hadn't minded the way the older woman snuggled up to Nick or that near lip lock. Much. But she wasn't going to let the countess score all the points. Deliberately, she let her glance drift to the egg-sized amethyst nestled between her hostess's breasts.

"Looks like you must be pretty good at what you do as well," she murmured.

A flicker of surprise crossed the countess's face before she threw back her head and let loose with a burst of raucous laughter. The earthy, snorting gusts should have diminished her air of sophistication. Oddly, they only underscored the woman's decidedly unique charm.

"Yes," she agreed after a moment, her eyes sparkling. "Yes, I am most decidedly good at what I do. Come, you must meet my friends."

Mackenzie had to admit the countess had collected a clutch of interesting friends. In the next few hours, she swapped sea yarns with a retired Turkish admiral, listened with delight to the wicked limericks tossed off by a cross-dressing poet laureate, and dodged several attempts by a slightly inebriated Olympic gold medal skier to feed her tidbits of smoked eel.

Meanwhile, the countess continued to claim her darling, darling Nick's attention. Ever adroit, he managed to keep her amused *and* appear at his "associate's" side often enough to resolve any doubts about their exact relationship. In the other guests' minds, anyway.

Mackenzie wasn't quite sure how the heck he managed to put his brand on her so effectively. He certainly didn't make any overt gesture, like draping his arm around her waist or tipping his champagne flute to her lips.

Maybe it was his lazy smile when he caught her eye from across the room. Or the word he dropped in the Olympian's ear when the skier became a little too persistent with the smoked eel. Or the admiring glances the emerald collar drew from the other women at the party.

"The stones are perfectly matched," a world-famous prima ballerina murmured, eyeing the necklace. "And so beautifully cut. Nick has such exquisite taste."

Sure that the dancer was going to recognize the piece as stolen at any moment, Mackenzie had a few silent words to say about Nick's taste. Her nervousness grew as the ballerina leaned forward and examined the emeralds. Mackenzie half expected her to pull a jeweler's loupe out of her evening bag.

Her swan-shaped evening bag.

"Wherever did Nick purchase this necklace?"

"You'll have to ask him," Mackenzie replied, her glance riveted on the beaded bag. "But first, you must tell me where *you* purchased that bag. I don't think I've ever seen one in that shape."

"I should hope not. It was designed exclusively for me, to commemorate my very first appearance at London's Royal Ballet. I debuted as Odile, the black swan."

Mackenzie arranged her face to look appropriately impressed as the dancer held the shimmering creation up for closer inspection.

"Every Marjorie Pelletier is individually crafted, you know."

"No, I didn't. Marjorie Pelletier, you say?"

"Yes." The ballerina stroked the beaded feathers lovingly. "Marjorie died some years ago, but her daughters continue her tradition of excellence. Their design studio is in Paris, but they have shops all over the world. There's one here in Nice, on the rue de France. You'll have to get Nick to take you there. Every woman should own a Marjorie Pelletier."

Particularly the well-kept mistress of someone as rich and generous as Nick Jensen, her tone implied.

"I will," Mackenzie murmured, accepting the futility of any attempt to set the record straight at this point. Excited about the possibility that she might have a lead on the butterfly-shaped bag Nick stole all those years ago, she went in search of him.

But when she circulated the salon, intending to inform him they had a shopping date, she discovered the man had disappeared on her.

Again.

This time, apparently, with the countess d'Ariancourt.

Common sense told Mackenzie to mingle and wait for Nick's return. Irritation that he would slip away without so much as a word had her reaching into her bag.

A flick of a switch activated the small, palm-size unit that received signals from the homing device she'd planted inside Nick's watch. Another flick set the receiver to silent, vibration-only mode. Closing her palm around the tracker, she slipped her hand inside the pocket of her wide, flaring palazzo pants and made another discreet circuit of the salon. The vibrations slowed at the far end of the cavernous room, where floor-to-ceiling widows opened onto the balmy night. They picked up again as Mackenzie approached a set of doors set midway along the west wall. Once through the doors, the device hummed steadily against her palm.

She meandered down a black-and-white tiled corridor hung with massive oils framed in ornate gilt. The vibrations remained constant until she reached a curved set of stairs. Sliding a hand along the milk-smooth marble balustrade, she started up the steps. The buzz increased in tempo.

One turn of the steps brought her level with a wide window embrasure. Mackenzie stopped short, her fist going tight on the tracker as she spotted a male figure leaning casually against the casement.

He was younger than most of the countess's guests, not more than twenty-four or -five. He was also, Mackenzie noted with a gulp, an Adonis. The stairwell's recessed lighting softened his chiseled cheekbones and firm jaw, but nothing could dim the impact of curly black hair, liquid brown eyes, and the most sensual mouth she'd ever seen on a male. Add a lean, muscled body that showed off his tux to perfection and he was enough to give any and all persons of the female persuasion heart palpitations. Mackenzie's certainly skipped a few beats.

He returned her scrutiny, smiling a little at what she suspected was the standard reaction to his masculine beauty. *"Recherchez-vous Dianthe?"*

She shook her head. "Sorry, I don't speak French."

"Ahhh. You are the American. Nick's...friend."

The delicate hesitation had her swallowing a sigh. She might as well have worn a flashing neon sign.

"And you are?"

"I am Alexander Danton." His beautiful mouth tipped up. "Dianthe's...friend."

"Oh. Oh, I see."

Good grief! The countess had to have at least two decades on this gorgeous creature.

Mackenzie gave herself a mental shake. If older men could amuse themselves with pretty young things, the same rules applied to older women. Which didn't explain why the countess kept her boy-toy hidden away, out of sight. Mackenzie was sure she hadn't met him downstairs. She would have remembered.

"Why didn't you come down and join the party?" she asked, curious.

His smile took a cynical twist. "Sooner or later, the party comes to me."

Yes, she supposed it did.

"Are you looking for Dianthe?" he asked. "She and Nick are upstairs, in the *petite salon*. Come, I'll show you."

The tracker vibrated wildly against Mackenzie's palm as he escorted her to the third floor. A long hallway ran the length of the house, with rooms opening off either side. A narrow carpet in lush jewel tones muted their footsteps as they made their way down the hall. It didn't, however, mute the low, throaty laughter that rippled from the second room on the right.

The door was partially open, showing a slice of another richly patterned carpet and walls hung with turquoise watered silk. Alexander pushed the door farther back. The same cynical smile that had twisted his mouth a few moments ago returned as he took in the sight of his mistress snuggled up against another man.

"Do we intrude, Dianthe?"

At his sardonic drawl, the countess glanced over her shoulder. She showed not the least discomposure at being found in a clinch.

Neither, damn him, did Nick!

His hands rested lightly on the countess's slim hips. His expression bland, he made no move to disengage.

Fury stabbed into Mackenzie—the same hot, searing wrath that had knifed through her when she'd discovered her ex in bed with their neighbor. Her hands curled into fists so tight the tracker's edges cut into her palm.

With the sharp stab of pain came an even sharper realization. Nick was *not* her husband. Not even the lover everyone here assumed he was. Mackenzie had no claim on him. None. Zero. Nada. A point she herself had reinforced several times, the latest being this very morning at the flower market.

So where the heck did this fury come from? This primitive urge to yank the countess's hair out by its salon-perfect roots? Thoroughly shaken by its intensity, Mackenzie realized she'd have to seriously reassess her feelings where Nick Jensen was concern.

The realization did *not* make the countess's trill of laughter any easier to swallow.

"Alexander, my pet. You've come to join us. And you've brought Mademoiselle Blair. How delicious! A ménage à trois is always so delightful, but four…"

She gave a little purr that set Mackenzie's teeth and won a grin from Nick.

"Behave yourself, Dianthe." Putting some distance between them, he raked a hand through his hair. "Now where is the painting you wanted to show me?"

With a careless hand, she gestured to a seascape hung above an escritoire. It depicted the Bay of Angels in colors that captured the very essence of the south of France. Golden yellow sunshine. Achingly blue water. Clean, white light contrasted with sharp shadows.

"The artist is little known," the countess commented, "but good, I think."

"*Very* good," Nick agreed, drawn to the painting. "His general opposition of light and dark areas to the exclusion of any halftones is very similar to Manet's later works. Astonishingly so."

"Perhaps that's why he's now in prison," his hostess said with another gurgle of laughter. "He claimed to have nothing to do with the fake Manet discovered in the Louvre's west gallery last year, but..."

Shaking her head in mock despair, she let her glance drift with seeming idleness to Mackenzie's glittering collar.

"Insurance company investigators have such unforgiving natures," she murmured. "They're worse than the police. My poor, struggling artist said they positively hounded him into a confession."

"Did they?"

Nick's reply was coolly unconcerned, but Mackenzie barely managed to refrain from slapping a palm over the emeralds. The nasty suspicion wormed into her mind that she and Alexander had interrupted more than a tryst. The countess's languid tale of the imprisoned artist and bloodthirsty insurance company inspectors sure sounded to her like a thinly veiled threat.

If it was, Nick didn't buy into it. Relaxed and amused, he strolled across the room.

"How like you to be on such intimate terms with an art forger, Dianthe. Shall we go back downstairs and rejoin the other guests?"

She waved a languid hand. "You go. You and your so delightful Mademoiselle Blair. Alexander and I shall follow in a while."

Or not, Mackenzie thought, taking in her companion's sardonic expression. Smothering a sensation of distaste along with the anger that still feathered just below the surface, she waited until she and Nick were on the stairs to voice her thoughts.

"That bit about the insurance companies sounded a whole lot like a threat to me."

His mouth curved. "It sounded very much like Dianthe to me."

"What are you saying? That Countess d'Ariancourt isn't above a touch of blackmail to keep her mouth shut about a certain stolen necklace?"

"I'd say there's very little Countess d'Ariancourt is above."

"Well, you should know."

She hadn't meant to let the acid seep into her voice…or let Nick know how much that little scene upstairs had gotten to her. She needed time to analyze the intensity of her reaction, needed space to understand why her head kept warning her away from Nick Jensen and her body kept ignoring the warnings.

The blasted man didn't give her either time *or* space to analyze anything. He halted a step down from her, eye level, blocking her way.

"You don't have to worry about Dianthe, Mackenzie. Or anyone else. I'm hanging loose until you decide whether you want to fan the sparks."

Her breath stuck in her throat. This morning, in the square, she'd been more than a little suspicious of the power he'd handed her with his casual promise to let her make the next move. Tonight, there was nothing casual in the way his blue eyes searched hers.

"One," she got out on a somewhat shaky laugh, "I'm not worried. Two, what I saw upstairs doesn't exactly fit my definition of hanging loose."

"What you saw upstairs was a game, one Dianthe is particularly adept at playing."

"No kidding. Just out of curiosity, what would you have done if Alexander or I had agreed to her suggestion of a frolicking free-for-all?"

"The same thing I did do. Hustle you right out of there." The glint in his blue eyes deepened. "I may move in what some people consider sophisticated circles, but there's more of the street tough left in me than I like to admit at times. I don't share, Mackenzie. My secrets or my woman.''

Good grief! And here she'd berated herself for the surge of primitive fury she'd experienced just moments ago at seeing another woman in Nick's arms. He was talking possession at its most elemental level, a man prepared to stake his claim and defend it against all comers.

The small corner of her heart still bruised from the bust-up of her marriage thrilled at the unequivocal statement. The rest of her pretty well got goose bumps, too. When Nick gave his word, he'd keep it. When he exchanged vows, he'd stick to them.

Except…

They weren't to the vow stage yet. They hadn't even jumped the first hurdle, namely moving this constant, irritating attraction out of the realm of the possible and into bed. She had to remember why they were here in Nice, she told herself, trying to suppress the shivery pleasure raised by the touch of his hand on her elbow. Had to remember, too, all the complications that would come when—*if!*— they crossed that invisible line between boss and subordinate.

Her heart pounding, she accompanied Nick down the stairs. Her pulse kicked up another few notches some time later when he suggested they leave. She nodded, her mind racing ahead to the hotel suite with its two monstrous beds.

They walked outside into the sea-scented night, Nick's hand at the small of Mackenzie's back. A warm breeze ruffled over her bare shoulders and back. Across the courtyard a short, stumpy figure detached himself from the cluster of chauffeurs blowing clouds of cigarette and cigar smoke.

"Back to the Negresco, sir?" Jean-Claude asked cheerfully.

"Yes."

Mackenzie slid onto the soft leather, wondering how in the heck she was going to make polite conversation with Nick during the long drive to the hotel when her skin still tingled from his touch and her imagination was working overtime. She couldn't stop thinking about what would happen if she struck that match Nick had talked about. Not even the sight of Nice strung out far below like a sparkling diamond necklace distracted her.

As it turned out, she didn't have time to make any conversation, polite or otherwise. The limo glided out of the courtyard and had barely begun the steep, winding descent when it suddenly picked up speed.

Through the thick Plexiglas separating the front seat from the rear, Mackenzie saw their driver's shoulders hunch. His arms jerked, fighting the wheel, while the back end of the limo fishtailed wildly around a sharp curve. The violent movement threw her against the door. She had a glimpse of a chasm of dark emptiness under her before the limo's rear end whipped back onto the tarmac.

Nick leaned forward, rapping out a query in French. The driver gave a strangled reply that escalated to a hoarse shout as he wrenched the wheel again.

His frantic action proved useless. The limo shot through a curve and sailed right off the road.

Chapter 9

"Omigod!"

Mackenzie got out only that one startled yelp before the limo went perpendicular. It tilted, hung in midair for an endless second or two, then slammed nose-first into the steep hillside.

Nick, leaning at an angle toward the Plexiglas divider, went crashing into it. Mackenzie grabbed at the handle above her door with one frantic hand and his pants leg with the other, hanging on to both for dear life as the limo's rear end hit with a teeth-jarring thud. She had time for one relieved breath, only one, before the vehicle began a plunging downward roll.

Tall slender poplars snapped off under its grill. Branches slashed at the darkened windows. Rocks tore at the undercarriage and crunched the sides, but nothing could stop the limo's lurching, uneven momentum. It just kept bouncing and rolling. Straight down. With the speed and force of a runaway freight train.

In those gut-clenching moments while tires flattened and trees whipped the windshield a sharp, stinging regret laced Mackenzie's panic. She'd had her chance with Nick. He'd laid the choice squarely in her hands as late as this morning. What a fool she was to listen to her head instead of her heart! What a blind, stubborn fool! They were going to die in a mangled mass of metal and chrome without once tasting the passion that simmered between them.

She was swallowing gulps of roiling fear and bitter regret when the limo collided with what Mackenzie sincerely hoped was an immovable object. The force of the impact sent Nick flying back. He slammed into her, nailing her against the leather seat. She couldn't move, couldn't breathe, until he climbed off her and wrenched open the door.

"This thing could flip or start rolling again at any second. We've got to get out."

She didn't need a second invitation. Panting, she scrambled out. Nick tried to help, but lost his footing on the steep slope and went down, taking her with him. Rocks scraped her bare arms and shredded her chiffon pants before Nick managed to halt his slide. His face a pale blur in the darkness, he grabbed at Mackenzie as she slid past and anchored her against the hillside. She lay under him, panting, her heart jackhammering against her ribs.

"Are you all right?"

"I think so." She made a few cautious moves. "No broken bones, anyway. How about you?"

"I'm okay."

Her heart still thudding, she twisted onto her back and craned upward for a glimpse of the limo. Its crumpled front end protruded out from the hillside like the prow of a ship. The boulder that had stopped its downward plunge groaned under its weight.

"Oh, God! Nick, we've got to get Jean-Claude out."

He was already clawing his way back up the slope. Mackenzie scrabbled behind him on all fours, unmindful of the sharp edges that sliced into her hands and knees. Cursing the wide-legged palazzo pants that caught the heels of her flimsy sandals, she fought to get her feet under her and aid Nick as he wrestled with the driver's door.

"Damn...thing's...jammed!"

The chauffeur lay slumped over the slowly deflating air bag. Mackenzie pounded on the window with the heel of her hand.

"Jean-Claude! Jean-Claude, can you hear me?"

He didn't move. Nick gave the mangled door another wrench. There was a hideous groan as metal scraped against metal, but gave only a few inches.

Suddenly, the limo shuddered. The boulder embedded in its grill tipped a few horrifying inches.

"We'll have to get him out the other side."

Terrified that the rock would give and the limo would plunge down to the sea with the unconscious driver still pinned against the wheel, Mackenzie scrambled around to the passenger side. She reached it before Nick and yanked at the door. Miraculously, it opened.

Not so miraculously, the violent movement affected the precarious balance between man and nature. The limo rocked again. The boulder groaned.

Realizing both were about to go, Mackenzie lunged across the front seat. Her frantic fingers closed around the driver's right arm at the same time Nick's fists wrapped around her ankle. With a ferocious yank, he dragged both her and Jean-Claude back across the leather seat.

They got him out mere seconds before the rock succumbed to the limo's weight. With a sudden crack, the boulder broke loose and tumbled down the hillside. The vehicle went with it. This time, though, the angle proved too steep and the limo flipped end over end.

Glass shattered. Metal shrieked. The sickening sounds ripped into the night until the darkness erupted. With a whooshing roar, flames leaped into the black sky. A blazing fireball, the limo continued its plunging descent until, finally, it came to rest. Hanging on to both Jean-Claude and their precarious perches on the slope, Mackenzie and Nick watched as the fire consumed what might well have been their coffin.

With the wreck still snapping and crackling, Nick carefully rolled the driver onto his back and felt for a pulse.

"He's alive. Barely. We need to get him immediate medical attention."

He fumbled in his pocket for the cigarette case that held a miniaturized, two-way transmitter. Even in the darkness, Mackenzie could see the silver case had been mangled by Nick's slide down the rocky slope. He tried to raise a signal a couple of times before tossing it aside. His mouth tight, he skimmed a glance down her bare shoulders and torn chiffon pants.

"You don't have your transmitter on you?"

"It was in my purse, and that went down with the limo." She hesitated for only a fraction of a second. "We have a backup system," she informed him tersely. "Give me your watch."

"My watch?"

"Hurry."

Frowning, Nick slipped the wafer thin timepiece from his wrist. Mackenzie used her fingernail to pry off the back. Chewing on her lower lip, she held the case up and tried to catch the faint glow of the moon. The damned device was so small and almost transparent, but she managed to find the pressure point that altered the signal. One squeeze, and it went from a random pulse to a continuous beat that the communications tech manning OMEGA's control center would recognize instantly.

Agent down. Send in the cavalry.

Fumbling the case back together, she passed the watch over Jean-Claude's still form. Shadows hid Nick's face, but there was no mistaking the edge to his voice when he inquired when she'd planted that particular gadget.

"This morning, while you were in the shower. I intended to remove it after our talk at the flower market, when we agreed we wouldn't keep any more secrets from each other. I got busy and forgot."

"Is there anything else you *forgot* to tell me?" The question sliced through the night like an ice-cold laser.

''Nothing I can think of at this particular moment,'' she retorted.

Nick got the message. His jaw snapped shut. With a look that promised they'd continue this discussion when they weren't perched above a flaming wreck, hanging on to a steep cliff by their fingernails, he worked his way out of his tux jacket and tossed it to her.

''Put it on.''

''I'm not cold.''

''Put it on, dammit. Your shoulders and arms are scraped and bleeding. It'll give you some protection if you slide down anymore.''

Until that moment Mackenzie hadn't felt any of her bumps and bruises. She became aware of every one of them, though, as she wiggled into the tux. Still warm from Nick's body, it wrapped around her like a blanket. Rolling up the cuffs, she reached over to help him loosen the chauffeur's tie and shirt collar. She knew better than to straighten his bent limbs, but the blood seeping from a laceration on his left temple worried her.

''He must have cracked his head against the side widow.''

Tearing a wide strip from her now-ragged slacks, Mackenzie folded it into a pad and pressed it against the wound. A scrabble of rocks on the other

side of his unconscious body told her Nick had decided not to wait for the cavalry.

"Stay with him," he ordered tersely. "I'm going
for help."

Mackenzie's eyes followed the white blur of his
shirt as he climbed slowly up the slope. He was
almost out of sight when she caught the distant wail
of a siren.

It was long past midnight before they returned to
the Negresco. With the poor driver in a coma and
the limo a smoldering wreck, the police would advance no theories yet as to the cause of the accident.

The Negresco's manager met his battered and
bandaged guests at the door. Called by the night
staff, who'd been informed of the accident by the
police, he'd pulled on his cutaway frock coat but
hadn't quite managed to knot his gray-striped silk
ascot.

"We are so distressed by this dreadful accident.
We'll take care of all expenses incident to your visit
to the hospital, of course."

Of course. Anything to avoid adverse publicity
or a possible lawsuit. Running his anxious gaze
over their assorted scrapes and bruises, he dogged
them across the lobby to the elevator.

"Please tell me, is there anything we can do to
ease your discomfort?"

"Send up a bottle of armagnac," Nick rapped out, stabbing at the up button. "1950 Chateau La Bataille."

"Yes, sir. An excellent choice, if I may say so. I believe… Yes, I'm sure we have a bottle in the cellar. I'll have it brought up immediately. And perhaps a tray of fruits and cheeses? Baked brie and some…?"

The elevator door swished shut, cutting him off in midcourse. Sighing, Mackenzie propped her shoulders against the burled walnut panels. With her dirt-streaked face, patchwork of gauze bandages and what was left of her bloodied pants showing below Nick's tux, she knew she looked worse than she felt, and she felt pretty grim. At least she hadn't lost the emeralds. Fingering the collar, she wondered whether their owner had ever experienced anything close to this heart-stopping excitement while decked out in the jewels.

Her pathetic appearance provoked little sympathy from Nick. When the door to their suite slammed behind them, Mackenzie took one look at the tight line to his jaw and abandoned any hopes they could retire to their separate bathrooms to wash up and change while they waited for the cognac.

"All right, let it out. You're still torqued about the tracking device in your watch, right?"

"Torqued doesn't begin to describe it. But that's not at the top of my list right now."

"What is?"

"You. I want you on the next plane out of Nice."

Stung, she jerked up her chin. "Why?"

"Because you could have died tonight," he snarled, startling her with his vehemence. "That's twice now you've dodged a bullet meant for me."

"So you don't believe our little adventure tonight was an accident?"

"Jean-Claude lost control of the car on almost the first turn. I doubt if there'll be enough left of the limo for a decisive finding, but no, I don't believe our little adventure tonight was an accident."

Mackenzie had entertained her own suspicions. Hearing them voiced aloud didn't make them any easier to swallow.

"We still don't know for sure you're the target," she argued. "It doesn't make sense for me to leave until… Hey!"

She'd forgotten how fast he could move. Closing the distance between them in two swift strides, he wrapped his hands around her upper arms and practically lifted her onto her toes.

"Don't you understand, you idiot? I don't want you used for target practice. Or sent over a cliff. Or burned alive at the bottom of a ravine."

"I'm not particularly keen on any of those options, either! But we're a team, Nick. We're in this together. We do this together or…''

His grip tightened. ''Or what?''

Obviously, the man didn't take kindly to threats, implied or otherwise. His combination of icy anger and savage concern for her safety reminded Mackenzie all too forcefully of her own wild swings of emotions. The fury when she'd spotted the countess wrapped around him. The jolt when she'd remembered she'd staked no claim on Nick that would keep the Dianthes of the world away from him. That heart-stopping moment after the limo nosedived off the cliff, when regret that she'd turned down Nick's offer tasted as bilious and as bitter as her choking fear.

Gulping, Mackenzie finally admitted the truth. Despite everything she'd done to keep Nick Jensen at a distance, the blasted man had gotten under her skin. Into her head. Around the barriers she'd erected to protect her heart. She didn't need another near-death experience to shatter her stubborn resistance. Or make her admit that some lines had to be crossed. She might regret this tomorrow, but tonight…

Tonight she had to touch him, taste him, take all he had to offer and give what was in her heart. With a little wrench, she pulled free of his hold.

"We're not finished here," he warned in a low growl.

"No, we're not."

Her pulse hammering, Mackenzie marched to the pedestal table set against the paneled wall. A Baccarat crystal ashtray sat on the table and held a book of matches encrusted with the hotel's seal in heavy gold foil. Her fingers closed around the matches. With a growing sense of absolute certainty, she faced Nick.

Bits of grass and leaves decorated his blond hair. Dirt streaked his white dress shirt. Unlike Mackenzie's, his slacks were still more or less intact, but she only now noticed that he'd lost one shoe. He looked tough and uncompromising and too damned impossible to resist any longer.

Her certainty leaped into hunger. With a thumping ache that had nothing to do with her scrapes or bruises, Mackenzie flipped up the embossed cover, struck a match and held the tiny flame up between thumb and forefinger.

"What the hell...?"

Confusion blanked Nick's face. He must have thought she was reacting to his burnt-alive crack. An apology was forming in his eyes when they suddenly narrowed. Mackenzie saw comprehension dawn in their blue depths and dredged up a shaky smile.

"You told me to strike a match when I'm ready, remember?"

"Yes."

She held his gaze above the tiny, dancing flame. "Tonight convinced me. I got my fingers burned once, but I don't want to go through life without ever feeling the heat again."

He didn't pounce. Nick wasn't the type. She saw his shoulders tense under the torn shirt, felt her own nerves coil as he absorbed her sudden change of heart.

"I seem to have missed something here. How did we get from putting you on the next plane out of Nice to playing with our own brand of fire?"

"I discovered I don't like seeing *you* used for target practice, either. And during our short, never-to-be-forgotten ride down from the countess's house, I realized I'd lied. To you and to myself."

The flame singed her fingertips. Hastily, Mackenzie dropped the match in the ashtray. The embers glowed a golden red, reflected many times over in the crystal. She pulled her gaze from the bright speck and met Nick's intent stare.

"I want what you offered me this morning at the flower market," she confessed with soul-searing honesty. "I've wanted it since my first weeks at OMEGA."

He was across the room almost before the words

were out. When he pulled her into his arms, Mackenzie wasn't sure which Nick to expect. The sophisticated charmer who'd raised goose bumps all over her flesh when he'd clasped the emeralds around her neck or the primitive male who'd pinned her to the carpet last night.

This Nick fell right somewhere between the two. He made no attempt to disguise his hunger, but he was careful of her bruises when he buried his fingers in her hair and angled her mouth up for his kiss. Mackenzie's lips opened under his. Her hunger mounting with each dart of tongue against tongue, she dug her fingers into his shoulders for balance as he backed her against the wall.

The hard press of his body set the spark to hers. After the terrifying plunge down the cliff, she needed this searing contact of warm flesh and eager mouths. She needed to feel this sudden surge of life, to let her blood rush wildly through her veins.

She needed Nick.

Her heart raced, pulsing with life, with greed, with desire. She angled her head to keep his mouth fused with hers while her hands splayed across his shoulders. His muscles bunched under her fingertips, hard and roped and all male.

Everything female in Mackenzie thrilled to the urgency he communicated with his mouth and hands. And to the efficiency with which he stripped her of his tux jacket and the tattered remnants of her evening wear.

Within moments, he had her down to her silk bikini panties, a few gauze bandages and the emerald collar. A little growl rattled around in the back of his throat as he ran his palm down her front, from her neck to her breasts to the hollow of her belly.

"This is how I imagined you when I pocketed that necklace the other night," he told her gruffly. "Your hair tumbling around your shoulders, your skin all flushed and hot, wearing only the emeralds."

His palm slid lower, yanked down her panties. Mackenzie didn't have any problem fulfilling his fantasy. After denying her desire for this man for so long, she burned for him.

Her head went back against the wall. Her mouth opened eagerly under his. Her breasts scraped his shirtfront, the nipples hard-tipped and aching. When he found her hot, wet center, every muscle below her waist clenched.

She almost climaxed then and there. Her eyes flew open. Desperate to quell the spiraling sensation, she jerked back.

"No!" she gasped. "Don't...end...it...yet."

Exerting an exquisite pressure on the slick, sensitive spot between her thighs, he brushed her mouth with his.

"Don't worry, Comm. This is just the beginning."

* * *

With the supreme vanity of all males, Nick had envisioned various scenarios for Mackenzie's eventual seduction.

None of those scenes included pinning her against a wall, with one of her calves hooked around his and her back arched while he used his hands and his mouth to wring a climax from her shuddering, rippling flesh. Yet Nick couldn't have stopped at that point if he'd wanted to, which he sure as hell didn't.

She was liquid incandescence, all bright, searing heat. She flamed around him, under him, her skin flushed with need, her mouth and hands as urgent as his. When she suddenly stiffened, a groan tearing loose from far back in her throat, raw male triumph slashed through him.

Only after the shudders died and she went limp against him did he carry her into the bedroom and stretch her out on the satin-covered duvet. He was already hard and aching, but her sensual sigh as she wiggled deeper into the feather-filled comforter and stretched her arms over her head came close to putting a permanent kink in his gut.

"That," she purred, "was wonderful. Just what every girl needs after sailing off a cliff." She eyed him from beneath her lids. "What about you, Nick? What do you need?"

"Give me ten seconds and I'll show you."

His watch went first. He tossed it on the bedside table with a sardonic reminder to himself to have Mackenzie debug it. Later. Peeling off his one shoe and socks, he attacked the silver studs in his white dress shirt. Impatience and the sight of Mackenzie's dusky-tipped breasts and full, swollen mouth had him ripping at the damned shirtfront. The studs popped and scattered. What was left of the fine-spun cotton shirt hit the floor. He'd just yanked down his zipper when a rap sounded on the sitting room door.

"Hell!" Frustration reddening his cheeks, Nick yanked the zipper up again. "That must be the armagnac. Don't move."

"Like I could right now."

Grinning at the wry response, Nick padded barefoot and bare-chested through the suite. His entire body was wire-tight and aching, but he withdrew a thin length of razor-edged steel from the sheath strapped to his ankle before putting an eye to the peephole. The blade remained nestled against the inside of his right wrist when he opened the door.

"Compliments of the management, monsieur. Fruit, cheeses, and..." Reverence filled his voice. "A bottle of 1950 Chateau La Bataille."

"Merci."

Relieving the waiter of his heavy silver tray, Nick promised to leave a hefty tip with the empty bottle and kicked the door shut in his face. The baked brie trailed a warm, yeasty scent as he carried the tray to the bedroom and deposited it on the table by the bed. The wicked blade slid down his wrist to lie beside it.

Mackenzie plucked a grape from the heaped bowl of fruit and popped it in her mouth, watching as he uncorked the squat, dust-streaked bottle. "What *is* armagnac, anyway?"

"A particularly fine cognac. This vintage is from the Grand Bas Armagnac region, west of here."

The bottle in his hand had probably been sold at auction and cost the equivalent of a midsize car. Smiling in carnal anticipation, he centered the bottle over Mackenzie's bare middle and tipped the neck.

"Nick!"

Laughing a protest, she hollowed her belly to keep the golden liquid from spilling onto the duvet. Laughter gave way to a breathless gasp when he set the bottle aside and stretched out beside her on the bed. Slowly, deliberately, he ran his tongue from her breasts to her belly. The cognac fired his taste buds, but Mackenzie's warm, rippling skin stirred the ravenous hunger he'd fought to keep under control until this point.

She tasted like nothing he'd ever imagined, and he'd woven more than a few erotic fantasies around this woman. Delicate, like a fine Chantilly crème. Salty in spots. Dark and warm and rich where the liquor dribbled down through the hair at the apex of her thighs.

He took his time, savoring her flavors, using his tongue and his teeth to stir his own appetites as well as hers. She was writhing when he rasped the last of the cognac from the inner folds of her slick flesh, panting when he rolled atop her. Positioning himself between her knees, Nick slid one arm under her waist to cant her hips.

Mackenzie didn't even try to delay the inevitable this time. She felt him slide into her. Felt her muscles stretching and pulling and clamping around him in tiny, exquisite spasms of pleasure. Determined to take him with her, she locked her ankles behind his thighs and matched him thrust for thrust.

"Mackenzie…"

The hoarse growl thrilled her to her core. He couldn't hold back. Had lost control. They were fused together. With a fierce stab of satisfaction, she clenched her muscles.

Chapter 10

Mackenzie drifted awake the next morning, confused by the weight draped over her waist and the unfamiliar sensation of being cradled against something solid and warm. Dreamlike images floated through her mind like fingers of morning mist. Glamorous gowns. Glittering flashes of green. Inky darkness shot with flames.

Muttering, she snuggled her bottom into the reassuring heat behind her. In response, the dead weight draped over her middle tightened. There was a rustle of sheets, a slide of cotton on cotton, and the hard platform under her thighs shifted.

"Morning, Comm."

The husky greeting pierced the last of her sleepy haze. Her eyes flew open. She took in the ornate armoire across the room, the sliver of bright sunlight slanting through drawn drapes, the remnants of Nick's white dress shirt tossed carelessly on the carpet.

Good grief! It wasn't a dream. None of it. Not the stolen necklace or the horrifying ride down the hillside or those mindless moments with her back to the wall and Nick at her front.

Having him behind her was almost as disconcerting as having him at her front. His chest hair tickled her shoulder blades. His muscled thighs rode high and hard under hers. And if that insistent prod at the back of *her* thigh was any indication, the man was a whole lot more awake than she was.

Desperately, she tried to sort through the conflicting demands of unbrushed teeth, a body sticky all over from several marathon sessions and a fully aroused Nick. She'd barely swiped her tongue over her fuzzy teeth when he eradicated all other considerations by the simple expedient of raising one knee, lifting her bottom a few inches and sliding into her.

Mackenzie let out a little breathless gasp at the invasion, another when Nick nipped at the lobe of her ear.

The toothbrush could wait.

* * *

Unfortunately, the rest of the world couldn't.

She was hanging on to another sheer precipice by her fingernails when a series of staccato beeps penetrated her screaming senses. Panting, she raised her head a few inches.

"Nick. The—the phone."

"Let it ring."

She caught another distinctive *beep-beepity-beep* and went stiff. "Wait a minute!"

Grunting, he obliged. Mackenzie gulped and fought to focus on something other than the rigid length of male suddenly gone still inside her. It took some doing.

"That's not the phone," she got out after some seconds. "It's my computer. Nick, my folks at OMEGA are trying to contact me."

With another small grunt, he withdrew and rolled to his side of the bed. Mackenzie scissor-kicked free of the tangled covers. Swaddling the top sheet around her, she trailed a train of fine Egyptian cotton as she rushed from the bedroom to the desk in the sitting room. A quick glance at the screen had her tapping in a coded response. A few seconds later, a gruff male voice came through the laptop's speakers.

"Sorry to buzz you so early, Chief."

She recognized her second-in-command instantly. "It's okay. What's up, John?"

"Plenty, evidently. That was some show last night."

Mackenzie barely bit back a choked exclamation. For a horrified moment, she wondered if she'd screwed up and set the surveillance cameras in the suite to relay live images from the hotel suite to the control center instead of feeding them only to her computer.

"Last night?" she echoed weakly.

"After you told us what happened and requested replacements for the transmitters lost in the limo, we tapped into the local police computers. Their report includes some real scary digitized on-scene pictures."

Sagging with relief, she realized he was talking about the near-fatal accident. *Not* what came after.

"I put the replacements for the equipment lost in the limo on a plane last night," John relayed. "You should get them within the next few hours. Also, I need to advise Lightning we've received a coded message from Ace. It's for his eyes only."

"Roger. He's in the other room. Hang loose and I'll go tell him."

"Tell me what?" Nick asked, striding through the bedroom door. He'd pulled on his wrinkled dress slacks, Mackenzie saw with a mixture of regret and relief. Starkly black against his tanned skin, they rode low on his hips as he crossed the room.

"Control's received a message from Ace, for your eyes only."

Swiftly, Nick moved to the computer. Mackenzie retreated to the sofa to give him the privacy required for these top-level communications. Bunching the cotton sheet around her breasts, she waited while he authorized transmission of the message. He was all business when he planted both palms on the desktop and skimmed the words that painted across the screen. Despite the bare feet, the uncombed hair, the stubble fuzzing his cheeks, he emanated an air of unquestioned authority he probably wasn't even aware of.

Mackenzie couldn't miss it, however. The lover who'd breathed erotic threats into her ear just moments ago had disappeared. This was Lightning. OMEGA's director.

Her boss.

With an inner grimace, she dragged the sheet up higher. She'd bet her next month's paycheck he'd start rapping out orders as soon as he finished reading the message.

She won the wager. His brows slashing down, Nick deleted the message and turned his frown on her.

"Ace thinks he might finally have a lead on the

Saudi oil field explosions. I need to advise the president. Set me up a secure channel.''

''Aye-aye, skipper!''

She would have whipped up a salute if it hadn't meant losing her grip on the sheet. Nick got the message, however, from the bite in her reply. Raking a hand through his hair, he softened the brusque order with a smile.

''It's still the middle of the night in Washington. Route me through the White House situation room, will you? I'll mark the message for the president's personal review. The senior rep on duty can decide whether to wake him or wait till morning.''

''Will do.''

They were both practically naked. Their bodies still carried the scent of their lovemaking. Yet Mackenzie knew Nick couldn't separate himself from Lightning, any more than she could put aside her responsibilities as OMEGA's chief of communications. Tumbling into bed together didn't necessarily mean equality out of it. He gave the orders. Mackenzie took them.

For now, anyway.

The thought sent a sharp spear of regret lancing through her. When she lit that match last night, she'd accepted the fact that there would be consequences. Now they were staring her right in the face.

She'd have to leave OMEGA. She couldn't stay. After last night, there was no way she could stay. If her years in the navy had taught her nothing else, it was that you didn't fool around with someone in your chain of command. Not if you placed any value on your job. Or your self-respect.

She'd *known* that, dammit. Had lectured Nick on the complications of an office affair not once, but twice. Then she'd tossed aside every hard-won lesson, every tenet of common sense and jumped his bones.

Which she'd do again.

In a heartbeat.

Sighing, she tucked the sheet under her armpits and edged Nick aside. Her fingers flew over the laptop's keyboard. It took only a few moments to make the link to the White House, a few more to arrange a secure channel to the situation room. A series of high-tech scramblers would encrypt the signals at either end of the channel and render the communication impervious to interception, much less decoding, by unauthorized sources.

Ordinarily, Mackenzie would have experienced a secret thrill at her ability to access the world's power centers. This morning, she felt only a dull satisfaction as she turned the computer over to Nick and retreated to her bedroom. He waited for the door to close behind her before sitting down to transmit his message.

Nick hit the send key and sprawled back in the striped satin armchair. He had a good idea of the president's reaction to Ace's startling tip that the Russians were somehow linked to Saudi oil field explosions. He wouldn't believe it, either.

Why in hell would the Russians want to blow up the refineries that provided them with a good percentage of their military and civilian fuel? It didn't make sense. Unless the destruction was the act of dissidents as intent on destroying what was left of the Soviet Union as some of the ultraright-wing, antigovernment hate groups in the States.

It always astounded Nick that those who schemed to bring down a government had little concern for the chaos that would follow. He'd come up against enough vicious, violent zealots during his years with OMEGA, though, to know they rarely looked beyond satisfaction of their immediate goals.

He tried to wrap his mind around the possibilities, searching the databank of his memory for some radical splinter group, some supranationalistic iconoclasts with the money and technical know-how to pull off the devastating series of explosions that had left a good chunk of Saudi Arabia blanketed in thick, black smoke. The faint drum of the shower coming from Mackenzie's bathroom kept getting in his way.

He pictured her naked. Her face tipped back to the stream. Water sluicing over shoulders and breasts. The need to finish what they'd started earlier brought him out of his chair. He was halfway across the room when the phone on the desk buzzed.

"My most sincere regrets for disturbing you so early," the hotel's on-duty manager said. "Inspector Picard from the Nice Prefecture of Police is here. She wishes to speak with you about last night's unfortunate incident."

Nick threw a tight glance at the door to Mackenzie's room and blew out a ragged breath. "Send her up. And a pot of coffee, with service for three."

"Oui, monsieur."

He used the next few moments to make a quick call to his contact in Europol to verify this Inspector Picard's credentials, then exchanged his wrinkled tux pants for crisply pressed gray slacks and a blue shirt in a soft blend of cotton and linen. Shoving his sockless feet into loafers, Nick opened the suite's door on the second knock.

His glance locked with that of a tall, slender female. She wore her auburn hair in stiff, gelled spikes that only someone with her incredible bone structure could carry off. Her gray eyes studied him through a screen of lashes inked a thick black.

"Monsieur Jensen?"

"Yes."

She flipped open a leather case to display her badge. In musically accented English, she identified herself. "I am Giselle Picard, deputy inspector with the Nice Prefecture of Police. I have been assigned to investigate the accident last night. May I have a few moments of your time?"

"Of course. Come in."

He half closed the door behind her, only to open it again as the elevator pinged and a waiter rolled off a service cart. It was the same waiter who'd delivered the cognac and cheeses last night, Nick saw. With a small, private smile, he waited for the man to wheel the cart into the suite, then reached into his pocket and extracted his money clip.

"Thank you. And I believe I still owe you a tip for delivering the cognac."

The server's eyes bulged at the bill Nick passed him. "Thank *you*, monsieur. Can I bring you anything else? Some fresh baked pastries. Some fruit?"

Nick looked to the inspector, who declined anything except coffee. The waiter made a show of pouring a rich black stream into blue china cups emblazoned in gold with the Negresco's logo, adding hot milk and sugar as requested, and passing the cups to Nick and Picard. The baroque silver pot hovered over the third cup.

"Will your, ah, companion be joining you, monsieur?"

"Yes, she will," Mackenzie answered, strolling into the room.

Her voice was composed, her manner polite as she sized up the newcomer. Nick tried to catch her eye and signal that he'd already vetted the inspector with Europol, but she didn't glance his way. In fact, she seemed to deliberately avoid looking at him.

She'd changed into white slacks and a silky, lime-green blouse with long sleeves that hid her scrapes and bruises. Her face was devoid of makeup, and she'd anchored hair still damp from her shower on top of her head with a plastic clip. She appeared cool and remote and all Nick could think about was pulling the clip from her hair and getting her naked again.

Shaking his head, he waited while the waiter softened the coffee's kick with a generous dollop of hot milk and handed Mackenzie her cup. When he departed, Nick made the necessary introductions. Inspector Picard wasted no time in confirming what they both already suspected.

"We've impounded the wrecked limousine, Monsieur Jensen, but our technicians advise that it's badly charred. They offer little hope of determining whether there was… How do you say? Mechanical failure.''

Mackenzie leaned forward, gripping the delicate china saucer. "What about Jean-Claude, our driver? Is he still hanging in there? Still clinging to life?" she amended at the inspector's blank look.

"He was when I left to come to the Negresco." Picard took a sip of her coffee and laid her cup aside. "I must tell you, however, that tests run at the hospital last night showed his blood alcohol count to be above the legal maximum."

"Oh, no!"

"The tests also showed traces of benzodiazephine. It is a commonly prescribed drug, but used incautiously it can cause dizziness, temporary paralysis and blackouts."

"Particularly when mixed with alcohol," Mackenzie muttered. She was certainly no expert, but she'd provided OMEGA's agents with enough information on the latest designer drugs and knockout drops to acquire a working knowledge of what interacted with what.

"Are you saying our driver was incapacitated and lost control of the vehicle?" she asked, dismayed by the thought. She liked Jean-Claude, had thoroughly enjoyed his tour-guide commentary and laid-back Niçoise attitude. She hadn't smelled alcohol on his breath last night, or noticed any slur in his speech.

"I say only that it is a possibility," Picard answered. "One of several we must consider."

"And the others?" Nick asked sharply.

Mackenzie gave the inspector full marks. Giselle Picard raised a penciled auburn brow at his peremptory tone and took her own sweet time answering.

"We understand Countess d'Ariancout's butler arranged for one of his underlings to serve refreshments to the limo drivers while they waited for their clients. That was, of course, mere courtesy. Still, we must not discount the possibility that someone slipped the drug into Jean-Claude's wine. One of the other drivers, perhaps. Or one of the staff. And we can't rule out the guests. I shall be interviewing them today."

Her gaze lanced into Nick.

"Was there anyone at the villa last night who might want you dead, Monsieur Jensen? You or Mademoiselle Blair?"

A short, charged silence descended, punctuated by the distant blare of horns of the morning traffic outside. Nick broke the tense quiet with a suggestion that she or her boss coordinate with Inspector Duarte, head of France's Europol office, before proceeding with this investigation.

Picard didn't appear to appreciate the suggestion. "Why is it necessary for my supervisor to coordinate with Europol?" she asked bluntly. "The incident occurred within the jurisdiction of the Nice prefect. This is my case."

"Not entirely. You can use the phone here, if you wish. Mademoiselle Blair and I will finish our coffee out on the terrace."

Mackenzie took the hint. Jurisdictional disputes could get ugly enough in the States, particularly with OMEGA's supersecret charter and direct line to the president. She had a feeling Giselle Picard was about to plunge into a political and diplomatic morass.

Drawn by the glorious vista of sea, beach and gently waving palms, Mackenzie rested her elbows on the stone balustrade. With such breath-stealing beauty spread out before her and the rich scent of jasmine perfuming the air, it took a conscious effort of will to remember the deadly hail of bullets that had brought her to the Côte d'Azur in the first place. Another to keep her expression neutral when Nick joined her at the railing.

Evidently she didn't keep it neutral enough. She felt his gaze on her face, heard the small chink as he placed his cup on the wide stone ledge.

"Got a problem, Comm?"

She turned to him then, her heart bumping at his

closeness. She could see the gold stubble fuzzing his chin and cheeks. See as well the speculation in his eyes.

This wasn't the time to tackle the thorny issue of where they went from here. They had a job to do. Unraveling the mystery of who was behind the attempts on Nick's life took precedent over everything else, including their dramatically altered relationship.

"What makes you think I have a problem?" she countered, making sure her jumbled thoughts didn't show on her face.

"This is the first time you've looked at me since you walked out of your bedroom," Nick said dryly. "I'm sensing a few morning-after regrets."

That at least she could respond to openly and honestly. "Oh, no. No regrets. I knew exactly what I was doing last night."

"So did I. And this morning."

That earned him a grin. "Too bad we didn't get to finish."

"We will." Smiling, he curled a knuckle under her chin and tipped her face to his. "Don't worry, Comm. We'll work this out."

She didn't see how. OMEGA had been her life for the past few years. Her home away from home after she'd left the navy. She couldn't imagine any job that would provide the same excitement, the same challenge to her skills. But neither could she see herself ping-ponging back and forth between the roles of subordinate and lover. She wasn't that good at compartmentalizing her emotions.

Nor could she allow her feelings for Nick to slop over into her job. She had too much professional pride for that. Something would have to give, and Mackenzie had a good idea what that something would be.

The door to the terrace opened at that moment, and one glance at Picard's stormy face told the story. Evidently, the inspector had not just plunged into a jurisdictional morass, she was totally ticked off by it.

''I am informed you and Mademoiselle Blair have been the subject of previous attacks,'' she said icily. ''And that Europol has been surveilling a telephone kiosk here in Nice, on the Avenue Jean Médecin.''

''That's correct.''

''I'm also informed that you will be present when I conduct my interviews of the countess's staff and the guests at her party last night.''

''I will.''

Mackenzie understood her anger. Getting an investigation yanked out from under you had to put a kink in your morning, not to mention your ego.

"Very well," the woman snapped. "Shall we go, then?"

"You go ahead," Mackenzie said when Nick turned to her. "John said he sent replacements for the equipment we lost last night. It should be here shortly. Then," she added, remembering the tip she'd received from the prima ballerina last night, "I might hit the shops on the rue de France."

Nick looked surprised, Giselle Picard impatient.

"I understand the boutiques carry all the best labels," Mackenzie murmured, unsure how much he wanted the inspector to know about his checkered past at this point. "Including hand-beaded evening bags by a designer by the name of Marjorie Pelletier."

Nick's quick frown mirrored Mackenzie's own jumbled thoughts. Obviously, he wasn't too thrilled at the idea of her wandering the city streets on her own. Yet they both knew she couldn't stay cooped up in the Negresco indefinitely, venturing out only when he was there to provide cover.

Still frowning, he reached out again and tipped her face to his. While the inspector fidgeted impatiently, Nick bent and brushed his lips across Mackenzie's.

"Be careful."

Fighting the ridiculous shivers raised by the touch of his mouth on hers, she nodded. "I will. Same goes for you."

Chapter 11

The promised equipment arrived just as Mackenzie was finishing a leisurely breakfast on the terrace. With the sun warming her shoulders and the bay sparkling an impossible turquoise, she checked out the miniaturized transmitter/receivers John had sent.

Nick's device was encased in a gold money clip this time. The box it came in bore the logo of a world-famous jeweler. Mackenzie didn't doubt the clip was eighteen karat gold. Nick Jensen wouldn't carry anything less. Smiling, she set the first box aside and opened the second.

Her device was embedded in an earring. The wide, beaten silver loop tugged at her earlobe, but the slight drag was worth the convenience. A casual hand to her nape, a careless flick of her hair, and her thumb activated an instant channel to OMEGA's control center. The crystalline clarity of the voice transmissions thrilled Mackenzie.

"You sound like you're standing right next to me," she gushed to John when he answered the signal. "Where did you get these devices?"

"From NASA. They're part of the new, robust microelectro-mechanical system the space gurus have developed for interplanetary communications. Those little hummers transfer tens of billions of bits per second using secure wireless networks and clusters of interlinked satellites. I volunteered you and Lightning to field-test the first units."

"I hope NASA doesn't plan on getting these babies back any time soon!"

"Careful, Chief. They might hear you. Hang on, I'll take you secure."

Satisfied that both units worked flawlessly, Mackenzie slipped on the other earring and dropped the box containing the gold money clip into her purse. She'd deliver it to Nick personally after her shopping expedition.

A half hour later, she decided that a stroll down the rue de France was something every woman should experience at least once in her life. She

wasn't much of a shopper, not one who would qual-
ify for a platinum credit card, anyway, but the restrained elegance of the shops lining the tree-shaded
boulevard almost made a convert of her.

Hermès. Chanel. Dior. St. Laurent. Lacroix.

All the famous French designers were represented, along with a host of Italians, Germans and
Americans. Mackenzie formed the distinct impres-
sion that anything that couldn't be found on the rue
de France wasn't worth buying.

She found the boutique she was looking for
tucked between a perfumery and a jewelry store displaying a single, diamond-studded pair of men's
cuff links in the window. The price tag accompa-
nying the links was small and discreet and carried
the same exclusive logo as the box in Mackenzie's
purse. Gulping at the amount listed in both euros
and francs on the tag, she entered the shop next
door.

"Bonjour, madame."

A saleswoman glided forward, her expert eye
taking in every aspect of her potential customer's
wardrobe and, apparently, her nationality.

"May I help you?" she continued in flawless English.

"Perhaps."

Mackenzie's gaze roamed the shop. The artistry
of the items displayed in the cases and on the

shelves took her breath away. The beadwork on
each piece was exquisite, the designs unique. She
couldn't quite see herself carrying an evening bag
in the shape of a roly-poly panda or a long-stemmed
white rose, but the shimmering, iridescent clam-
shaped number dangling from a braided black silk
cord roused an instant, greedy longing in her breast.
One glimpse of the price discreetly displayed next
to the bag had her wrenching her gaze back to the
saleswoman.

"I met a woman last night, a prima ballerina. She
was carrying one of your bags. A black swan."

"Ah, yes. That was one of Marjorie's later designs. It's quite famous."

"Is it?"

"Madame Pelletier's daughters featured it in
their book about their mother and her work." Smiling, she gestured to the lavish edition resting on a
glass-topped table. "Would you like to leaf through
it? I'll bring you some coffee, yes? Or champagne?"

"Coffee, please. With milk."

Mackenzie settled in a tufted white chair and
pulled the heavy volume toward her. She knew it
wouldn't be this easy, didn't really expect to flip
open the fly leaf and find a butterfly-shaped design
staring her in the face. Still, she couldn't suppress

a tingling sense of anticipation as she leafed through the pages.

Familiar faces gazed back at her from every page. Brigitte Bardot, who'd made the Riviera her private playground. Wallis Warfield Simpson, the duchess of Windsor. Even the notoriously dowdy Mamie Eisenhower was there, beaming at the camera as she displayed her tasseled, fan-shaped original.

The designs became more exotic as the forties and fifties gave way to the sixties and seventies. So did the customers. Mackenzie recognized an American starlet who'd traded Hollywood for a veil and marriage to a Middle Eastern prince, as well as the world-renowned animal-behaviorist who carried a beaded orangutan slung over one rather muscular shoulder. Grinning at the similarity between the purse and its owner, Mackenzie sipped her coffee and skimmed the rest of the book. She found the ballerina and her black swan, but no butterfly.

"That's quite a collection," she remarked, deciding on a direct approach. "I'm something of an amateur entomologist myself. Did Madame Pelletier or her daughters do any designs in the shape of bugs?"

"But of course."

Smiling, the saleswoman retreated behind a counter and withdrew a box bearing the shop's distinctive logo. Nestled inside was a ladybug in glistening red and black.

"It's beautiful, but I was thinking more along the lines of a butterfly."

"Ahh, yes. Madame Pelletier did several variations of *le papillon*. Her daughters also. But none, I think are as beautiful as the first. It was quite, quite lovely. So sad that it was lost."

Mackenzie's pulse tripped. "Lost?"

"It was stolen years ago. The countess was very distraught."

Excitement burst like bubbles in her veins. Hiding it behind a bland look, she probed for more information.

"Would that by any chance be Countess d'Ariancourt?"

"Yes. Do you know her?"

"I attended a party at her villa last night. How unfortunate that she lost one of these beautiful creations."

And how interesting!

"I understand it was a gift to her from one of her many, ah, admirers," the saleslady volunteered. "She used to call or come by the shop occasionally to see if it had surfaced. If anyone had been photographed with it, or been seen carrying it, we might have been able to verify that the bag belonged to her. Each piece is numbered, you understand."

"You say she used to call or come by. Not any-more?"

"I haven't heard from her in some months. After so many years, one can only assume she gave up hope of having the bag returned."

Or she finally tracked it down to a pawnshop in Cannes, Mackenzie thought on a spike of sheer adrenaline. She couldn't figure the connection be-tween the stolen purse and the recent attacks on her and Nick, but she'd bet her last dime there was one. There had to be one.

Anxious to get to Nick, she started for the door. "Thanks for the coffee. I've got to go."

"Don't you wish to see our latest catalogue? It features a variation of the butterfly design that…"

"Sorry. I don't have time now. Perhaps later."

"*Bien.*" Too well-mannered to show regret at losing a fat commission, the clerk smiled and wished her a good day.

Once outside, Mackenzie slid on her oversize sunglasses and played with her earring. Mere mo-ments later, her second-in-command's hearty voice filled her ear.

"Control here. What do you need, Chief?"

"The street address of Countess d'Ariancourt."

She remembered it was located off the twisting road called the Upper Corniche, but needed something more than that to give a taxi driver. John came back with the requested information a few seconds later.

Hailing a cab, she gave him the address and settled back on worn leather seats smelling of garlic and cigarette smoke. Of all the times not to be in direct communication with Nick. Was he still at the villa, interviewing the staff? Or had he and the inspector moved on to the guests? With a distinct feeling of regret that she'd removed the tracking device from his watch, she watched the red tile roofs of the city drop below the cab and tried not to think about the last time she'd traveled this narrow, winding road.

The countess's butler met Mackenzie at the door. His face set in rigidly disapproving lines, he related that Monsieur Jensen and Inspector Picard had departed the premises some fifteen minutes ago.

"Mademoiselle must have passed them on the drive up," he said with something close to a sniff. Evidently the man didn't appreciate being questioned by the police.

Mackenzie eyed the taxi she'd kept waiting and made a spur-of-the-moment decision. "Is the countess at home? I'd like to speak with her."

"If you'll wait in the downstairs salon, I'll see if madame wishes to receive you."

Not exactly a gracious welcome, considering that two of madame's guests had nearly been splattered down a steep slope not far from here. Nick and Inspector Picard must have raked the man and his underlings over the coals.

After paying off the cabdriver, Mackenzie followed the majordomo into a cozy, irregularly shaped room just off the downstairs hall. It was tiled in black and white, with an elegantly faded area rug to absorb the echoes, and furnished in dark woods. A glass-fronted armoire held a collection of Fabergé eggs, some small, some ostrich-size, each on its own stand. Mackenzie was admiring one done in glowing red and navy cloisonné when the sound of footsteps in the hall announced the countess's arrival.

It wasn't the petite, raven-haired aristocrat who strolled into the salon, however, but her companion. His stunning male beauty hit Mackenzie all over again, almost like a smack to the face. She blinked, reared back a little, and let out a slow breath.

Damn! The way this gorgeous creature had filled out his tux last night was mind-boggling enough. That was nothing compared to hot and sweaty and just off the tennis courts. His white knit shirt clung to his chest and muscular shoulders in damp spots. His shorts...

Mackenzie had seen shorter shorts on a man, but he'd been suspended over the side of a navy cruiser at the time, struggling to fix a navigational beacon under the broiling equatorial sun. She suspected the countess must have chosen this tennis ensemble for her companion with the sole intention of showing off his trim, tight butt.

"Mademoiselle Blair!"

Tossing his tennis racket onto a chair, he came across the room. "You look well," he murmured, brushing his mouth across the backs of her fingers, "for having so narrowly escaped death last night."

Strange how the slightest touch of Nick's mouth on her flesh started small eruptions of heat just under her skin, yet Alexander's kiss left her stone-cold. Tugging her hand free, she shrugged off her lacerated knees and elbows.

"I got a few scrapes, but nothing a few Band-Aids and Mercurochrome couldn't fix. Unlike our driver," she added. "He's still in a coma."

"So I've heard." His black, liquid eyes held hers. "He has not spoken, then? Said what happened?"

"No."

"A police inspector was just here, I'm told. And

your friend, Nick. The idea that any of her staff or guests might have slipped your driver a drink or some drugs will no doubt be upsetting to Dianthe.''

The countess would probably be even more upset if the purse a young, sticky-fingered Nick stole from her years ago turned out to have some connection to a murderous attack by two gunmen.

Mackenzie thought momentarily about mentioning the evening bag to Alexander. Just as quickly, she discarded the idea. For one thing, he would have been in diapers when the theft occurred. For another, she hadn't had time to run a background check on this guy and find out just where he was coming from.

He gave her a hint at that moment, moving in closer.

Too close.

Mackenzie held her ground, but she didn't care for the way his combination of musky cologne and healthy male sweat teased her nostrils. Nor did she like the sudden intensity in his dark, penetrating gaze.

''Who are you, Mademoiselle Blair? What is your connection to Nick Jensen?''

''I thought we established that last night,'' she returned coolly.

''Ah, yes. You say you are his…friend.''

And then some.

The searing memory of Nick tipping cognac onto her stomach had put a whole new spin on the term friendship. To Mackenzie's consternation, her muscles tightened at the remembered rasp of his tongue on her belly. Desperately, she tried not to think about the other spots he'd rasped. Despite her best efforts, heat warmed her chest and stained her cheeks.

For Pete's sake! She couldn't believe she was standing knee-to-knee with the countess's latest lover and blushing like a teenager. Nor could the countess when she sailed into the salon some moments later.

In an ironic reversal of roles from the night before, the black-haired, flawlessly madeup aristocrat interrupted what had all the earmarks of an intimate tête-à-tête. Her young stud leaned over Mackenzie, intent and intense. She stared up at him, no doubt looking as flustered as a fifteen-year-old after her first real make-out session.

"Well!" The countess stopped on the threshold, her eyes widening. "Have you changed your mind, Mademoiselle Blair?"

"About what?"

"About joining Alexander and me in a little frolic?"

"Sorry. I'm not into frolics."

Not with these two, anyway. The idea of getting naked and indulging in some afternoon delight with Nick, on the other hand, held a definite appeal.

A malicious smile curved the countess's lips as she strolled across the room. Running a red-tipped nail down her lover's arm, she wrinkled her nose.

"You're so deliciously sweaty, my pet. Did you work up that manly stink on the tennis court? Or here, with Mademoiselle Blair?"

"You heard her. She's not interested in the kind of games we play, Dianthe." His mouth took on a twist every bit as cruel as his mistress's. "Nor should she be. She has the look of a woman well loved this morning, does she not?"

The countess threw Mackenzie another look. Her lips thinned for a moment before pursing into a pout.

"Indeed she does."

"Or perhaps that's not whisker burn on her neck and chin," Alexander continued, his gaze still dark and intent. "Mademoiselle Blair indicated she took some bad scrapes when she tumbled down the slope last night."

"Such a dreadful accident!" Oozing concern, the older woman crossed the room and hooked her arm in his. "We heard the explosion here at the villa. I was sure a gas main had gone up, wasn't I, my pet? That happened only last month," she went on, not waiting for his answer, "down in the Old City. Several people were injured. But this…"

A shudder rippled down her slender frame.

"This is so much worse. My darling Nick could have been killed. You, too, of course."

Witch, Mackenzie thought. She could at least *try* for a little less insincerity.

"Did you wish to speak to me about the accident?" the countess asked solicitously. "Nick has already done so. He and a police inspector." Her glance shifted to the man beside her. "Too bad you missed them, my sweet. Someone on the staff mentioned that you issued the order for more refreshments to be served to the waiting drivers. That seemed to interest the police inspector."

"Did it?"

"I explained to her that you're always so thoughtful. And so thorough."

"Yes, I am."

The hair on the back of Mackenzie's neck prickled. She sensed undercurrents swirling around her, deep and more than a little dangerous. Swiftly, she jettisoned the idea of querying the countess about her stolen bag.

"Since you've already spoken with Nick and the

police inspector, I won't take up any more of your time.''

She started for the door, only to have the countess disengage her arm from Alexander's and glide into her path.

''You mustn't run off so quickly. Stay and have lunch with us.''

''Thanks, but I...''

''I'm afraid we must insist.''

She sensed rather than saw the movement behind her. Whirling, she read the intent on Alexander's face. Her arm came up in an instinctive move to shove him away.

His caught her wrist and wrenched it behind her back. Pain shot up her arm as he jerked her against him, pinning her hard against his chest.

Mackenzie could have sworn she caught a flash of regret in his dark eyes, but by then both anger and adrenaline had kicked in. With a smothered curse, she brought her knee straight up.

He twisted sideways just in time. Snarling, she bent her upper body back as far as the brutal hold on her wrist would permit. A head butt would hurt her almost as much as it did him, but she was damned if she'd let these two play their games without putting up a good fight.

Before she could smash her forehead into Alexander's nose, something sharp bit into her upper arm. Twisting, she shot a look over her shoulder and saw the countess plunge down the stem of a syringe.

"What is that? What did you give me?"

"Nothing *too* debilitating, darling."

"Benzodiazephine. Is that benzodiazephine?"

The older woman merely smiled. Mackenzie managed one last curse before the room began to blur and her knees went out from under her.

Chapter 12

When Nick returned to the Negresco just past two that afternoon, the concierge handed him an embossed envelope. The heavy vellum gave off a whiff of lavender as he unfolded the enclosed note and skimmed the bold script.

Darling—
Join us for cocktails on the *Sea Nymph*. We'll cruise the bay and watch the sun set. Mackenzie's already aboard. Call the harbormaster, and we'll send the skiff in to pick you up.

D.

Strange that Mackenzie hadn't left word that

she'd gone for cocktails with Dianthe, Nick mused
after letting himself into their suite and taking a
quick glance around. Stranger still that she hadn't
made arrangements to get him the replacement for
his smashed transmitter. He saw the box, which
confirmed the equipment had arrived, but no sign
of the new devices.

Tossing his key and Dianthe's note onto the desk,
he booted up the laptop computer and connected to
OMEGA's control center. The young, bright face
of Mackenzie's latest recruit—a math wizard right
out of MIT—flashed onto the screen. After verify-
ing Nick's voice and digital face prints, she
matched them to the authorization code he keyed
in.

"Control here. Go ahead, Lightning."

"Just checking in. What's happening?"

"Not much, sir. We received a sit rep from the
CIA indicating a potential anti-American demon-
stration in Singapore, but other than that it's been
quiet."

"Any word from Ace?"

"No, sir."

"How about Comm?"

"The chief?" A puzzled look crossed the communication tech's face. "I don't have her on my
status log. Was she supposed to report in?"

"No. I just wondered if you'd heard from her."

"No, sir. Do you want me to contact her?"

OMEGA's standard headquarters operating procedure was to avoid contacting operatives in the field unless absolutely necessary. Too often the agents found themselves in extremely tight spots. A signal from headquarters at the wrong time, even a silent signal, could blow their cover.

Mackenzie wasn't an operative, of course, but Nick's training and experience went too deep to violate procedures without justification. His stinging disappointment at not finding Mackenzie stretched out on the bed, eager to finish what they'd started this morning, didn't exactly pass the test for justifiable necessity.

"No," he instructed the tech, "don't contact her. I'll be seeing her shortly. In the meantime, run a background check on an Alexander Danton. Age approximately twenty-five. Black hair. Black eyes. No visible scars or tattoos. Occupation…"

The countess's staff had offered wildly divergent opinions about her young companion's interests, tastes and lack of any discernible source of income. Their employer usually chose lovers who lavished her with gifts, not the other way around. The staff's avid speculation about the man's past had piqued Giselle Picard's interest…as had the fact that he'd apparently issued the order to serve the waiting drivers another round of refreshments. Giselle intended to run a background investigation on Danton and return to the countess's villa to interview him. Nick would augment her data with whatever OMEGA could dig up on the man...and what he finessed out of Dianthe during cocktails aboard her yacht this afternoon.

"Occupation unknown," he finished. "Sorry I don't have more for you to go on."

"No sweat, sir. I'll get back to you as soon as I have something."

Nick signed off and clicked down the computer's lid. Drawn by the dazzling white light, he went out onto the terrace. He felt edgy and frustrated, and not just by Mackenzie's unexpected absence. Things were moving too fast...and too slow.

He'd been in Nice for three days. He should have established a link to the shootings in D.C. by now. He sure as hell should have experienced some warning, some sense of danger before he and Mackenzie climbed into that limo last night. His instincts had never failed him so completely before.

Frowning, he narrowed his eyes against the glare of the sun off the sea and searched the bay. Sailboats scudded with the wind, weaving through the yachts bobbing at the end of their anchor chains. He thought he identified Dianthe's *Sea Nymph,* a sleek triple-decker purchased for her years ago by one of her wealthier lovers. Nick had only been aboard once before, to attend a reception for the Belgian minister of defense. The man had fawned all over Dianthe, downed far too much champagne and ended up hanging over the side, spewing out his guts—not particularly wise or admirable behavior for a minister entrusted with a briefcase full of NATO secrets.

Still frowning, Nick retreated inside the suite to trade his loafers for rubber-soled deck shoes. His navy blazer looked jaunty and nautical enough for cocktails aboard the *Sea Nymph*. It also provided more than adequate cover for the leather scabbard he strapped to his forearm. He flicked his wrist, smiling grimly as a thin, tensile length of steel slid past his fingers. Those same fingers closed instinctively around the blade's handle.

Satisfied that he hadn't lost his touch, he slipped the stiletto back into its scabbard and left the hotel. Twenty minutes later, he walked out onto the stone quay and hailed a water taxi.

An annoying *whump, whump, whump* dragged Mackenzie from sleep. She woke to a fierce headache and a mouth that felt as though it was stuffed with cotton balls. Running her tongue over dry lips, she pried open first one lid, then the other. Fuzzy shapes danced in front of her eyes, gradually took on definition.

Frowning, she stared at the wild creature staring right back at her. The woman's hair fanned out in a dark halo above her head. Her clothes were wrinkled and twisted, with a tail of her blouse hanging out the waistband of her white slacks.

Mackenzie blinked, trying to clear the haze swirling around in her head, and realized that wild-looking creature was her. She lay flat on her back, spread-eagle on a bed that rocked gently, staring at her reflection in a mirrored ceiling.

Gulping, she twisted her head to one side. The room she was in looked sleekly modern, with walls paneled in light oak and exquisitely cut Art Deco fixtures. Piercing white light streamed through a round window set high in the opposite wall, adding to the ache inside her skull.

There was another small *whump,* and the bed under her rocked again.

A boat. She was on a boat. Those were waves slapping against the side, causing that little roll. And the round window was a porthole, perfectly positioned to let in the damned glare. Groaning, Mackenzie lifted a hand to shield her eyes. Or tried to.

There was a muffled rattle, and her arm jerked to a halt mere inches off the pillow.

"What the…?"

She tugged again, scowling when she got the same result. It took another moment for the last of the fog to clear. Only then did it sink in that her wrists were encased in leather cuffs and restrained by short lengths of gleaming silver chain. So, she discovered a moment later, were her ankles.

Craning her neck, she stared down at her widespread legs in disbelief, in disgust, in swift, searing fury.

The countess!

Damn her all to hell and back.

She must have decided to forcibly overrule Mackenzie's objections to participating in her kinky sex games. Yanking at the cuffs again, she let loose with a colorful stream of curses that would have done her old buddies in the navy proud.

In almost the next breath fury gave way to cold reality. Dianthe had to know Mackenzie wouldn't put up with being drugged and chained, that she'd raise holy hell when released. Obviously, the countess intended to ensure her silence…one way or another.

Memories of the previous night's near fatal accident came rushing back. She didn't need hard evidence to now believe Jean-Claude had been deliberately drugged. The countess was playing for

keeps, and her games involved more than per-
verted sex.

Flopping back down on the bed, Mackenzie
tested the chains again, this time with grim determination. Gritting her teeth, she grunted and
strained and almost dislocated her left shoulder in
a futile attempt to snap one of the links.

The sound of muffled voices put an end to her
struggles. She went still, her gaze on the door as it
opened.

"*C'est bien.* You are awake."

Countess d'Ariancourt flowed into the room,
trailing pale mauve silk and the scent of lavender.
Alexander followed. His gaze unreadable, he surveyed the figure spread-eagle on the bed.

Mackenzie's jaw tightened. She'd be a long time
forgiving herself for letting these two take her down
without a fight.

"Yes, I'm awake. And not particularly happy at
the moment."

The countess took malicious delight in the sparks
shooting from her captive's eyes. Oozing false sympathy, she made a small clicking sound.

"I know, I know. So humiliating to find oneself
helpless, is it not? And so deliciously erotic."

"Only for someone too jaded...or too old...to

get their jollies any other way,'' Mackenzie oozed back.

''Oooh la la! She's most definitely regained her bite, has she not, Alexander? What a pity we have no time now to show her the other toys in our little love nest. Later, perhaps. After Nicolas arrives.''

''Nick's coming?''

''But of course. I sent him a note, informing him you were already aboard.'' Her violet eyes gleamed in anticipation. ''He's joining us for cocktails.''

Mackenzie's stomach knotted. She didn't appreciate being used as bait any more than she appreciated being restrained. These two would most definitely answer for both.

''The harbormaster just radioed to let us know a water taxi's on the way,'' Alexander advised her. ''Until it gets here, I would suggest you don't hurt yourself by straining against the chains. They won't give.''

She made no effort to hide her disgust. ''Tested them yourself, have you?''

''We saw you testing them.''

With a sardonic twist of his lips, he gestured to the mirror above the bed.

''There is a camera. It feeds into the TV in the main salon. Dianthe enjoys watching almost as much as participating.''

"Why doesn't that surprise me?"

Smiling at her sarcastic drawl, he reached for the door handle and ushered his mistress out of the cabin. Mackenzie caught a glimpse of the wood-paneled companionway beyond before the door shut and she was left alone to glare up at the mirror.

Okay. All right. The camera bothered her, but not as much as the fact that she couldn't reach the earring gleaming wide and silver against her out-flung hair.

There it was, a direct satellite link to OMEGA's control center just inches from her fingertips. Maybe if she hunched and caught the earring between shoulder and lobe, or twisted her neck and dragged its back against the spread....

Neither contortion activated the transmitter. Hoping the camera would record a woman trying desperately to writhe free of her bonds, she tried several more maneuvers. Her breath came in shallow pants and her shoulder joints ached before she finally admitted defeat.

She'd have to wait for Nick.

Everything in her cringed at the thought. Unlike the countess, she didn't find being helpless the least stimulating or erotic. She hated the idea of being staked out like some Victorian virgin tied to the tracks, needing rescue. Hated even more the idea that the countess had used her as bait to lure Nick into a trap. He wouldn't know what he was walking into. He couldn't. The replacement for his communications device was still in Mackenzie's purse.

Which, she noted after a quick glance around the cabin, was sitting on the built-in nightstand beside the bed. The countess or her boy-toy had dumped the contents out onto the stand. They lay in a small heap. Her compact. Her lipstick. Her wallet. Her sunglasses. The jeweler's box with the embossed gold logo.

Her pulse jumped.

They'd opened the box, checked out the money clip. It sat loosely in its satin nest, almost—*almost!*—within reach.

Heart pounding, she scrunched toward the side of the bed. The chain anchoring her right arm went taut. The cuff bit into her wrist. Ignoring the pain, she groped for the box with her left hand. All she needed was another inch or two....

Grunting, she forced straining muscles to stretch farther. Her shoulder joint registered a sharp, stabbing protest. Closing her mind to the hurt, she sucked in a deep breath and put everything she had left into a small lunge. Her eyes watered with the pain, but she managed to hook her index finger on the box. It flipped up and the money clip tipped out, landing within easy reach.

"Yes!"

Excited by her victory, she almost forgot the camera hidden behind the mirror. With her fingers wrapped around the gold clip, she figured she'd better play the scene for all it was worth.

"This is Nick's," she hissed, glaring up at the mirror. "I bought it for him this morning on the rue de France. I'll be damned if your little pet is going to have it, Dianthe."

Sliding her thumb along the back of the clip, she activated a satellite link. The words tumbled out in an urgent attempt to keep OMEGA's control center from coming on line and acknowledging her signal.

"You think you can keep me chained here, on your boat? Not hardly, Countess. Nick will have something to say about all this when his water taxi arrives in a few minutes. He's not going to appreciate the fact that you drugged me and, apparently, our limo driver last night. Nick didn't enjoy going off that cliff any more than I did."

Mackenzie thought she heard the hum of an approaching engine. Gulping, she rushed on.

"Or are you planning to drug him, too? Arrange another accident? A drowning this time? You won't get away with it, you know. Inspector Picard from the Nice Prefecture of Police is on the case. She won't buy another accident.''

That was definitely an engine. It was louder now, closer. Suddenly, the muted roar died. The launch must be angling in, positioning to deliver its passenger. Slicking her tongue along her lips, Mackenzie kept up her desperate monologue.

"Picard will find out soon enough that Nick hired a water taxi. In fact, I wouldn't be surprised if she isn't tailing him, just to see where he's headed. She's probably right behind him. Or watching through high-powered binoculars.''

She couldn't broadcast a plainer message. It was time to send in the cavalry. Again. She could only hope whoever was manning the control center had the sense not to acknowledge her transmission.

To her infinite relief, the on-duty controller kept silent. At least, Mackenzie hoped that explained the lack of response. Surely the transmitter was working. She'd tested it herself this morning. God, she hoped she'd keyed it properly before pouring out all that babble!

She had no time now to stew about whether or not her transmission had gone through. The hollow tread of footsteps sounded again in the corridor outside the stateroom. Closing her fist around the money clip, Mackenzie tensed.

Alexander entered. His dark eyes inscrutable, he moved to the head of the bed.

"Nick's here. Dianthe wants you upstairs."

"So she sent her trained dog to retrieve me. Do you always sit up and bark at her command?"

The taunt brought a cynical smile. "Always."

Craning her neck, Mackenzie watched him hunker down beside the bed. The chain anchoring her right wrist came loose with a silvery tinkle.

She coiled her muscles. One solid clip to the jaw. That's all she figured she'd get in. She'd have to time it just right, use every bit of leverage she could manage with both ankles still anchored...

Alexander preempted any and all moves. Wrapping the loosened chain around his fist to keep it taut and Mackenzie contorted at an awkward angle, he rounded the foot of the bed. In a matter of moments, he had both wrists behind her and banded together. Only then did he release her ankles. To her profound disgust, he took care to stay well out of kick range.

"Be careful," he warned when she swung her feet over the side of the bed and struggled into a sitting position. "The drug may still be in your system. And you won't have your sea legs yet."

"I can't tell you how much I appreciate your concern!"

"Let me help you."

She jerked away from his outstretched hand, snarling. "Touch me again, and one of us won't live to regret it."

The issue hung in the balance for several moments before Alexander flicked a glance at the mirror above the bed.

"We've provided enough entertainment for Dianthe and Nick, Mademoiselle Blair. I've no doubt they're both thoroughly enjoying the show. Let's go up to the main salon and join them, shall we?"

Chapter 13

Dianthe and Nick?

Enjoying the show?

The sardonic comments echoed in Mackenzie's head as she made her unsteady way down the companionway. As Alexander had predicted, her legs felt spongy and her stomach had a tendency to lurch with every roll of the ship. The slight queasiness didn't bother her as much as the insidious doubts Alexander had planted, though.

Surely Nick and the countess weren't in this together—whatever "this" was. No way Lightning would have allowed that witch and her playmate to dope and shanghai OMEGA's chief of communications.

Why not? a nasty little voice countered. OMEGA's chief of communications had zapped Lightning with a Taser just a few nights ago. Maybe he was just getting some of his own back.

This was crazy! Mackenzie couldn't believe she was even considering the possibility that Nick and the countess shared anything more than a passing acquaintance and a possible link through an evening bag stolen years ago. It had to be the drug making her think so crazy.

Or so she tried to convince herself as she climbed the circular staircase leading to what was obviously the main deck. Instead of portholes, tall glass windows let in the afternoon sunlight and illuminated a series of salons all done in '30s era Art Deco. The dining room was a symphony in white and black, with sixteen chairs grouped around a glass-topped table crowned with a vase of calla lilies. The mirrored bar in the middle salon contained a cozy grouping of armchairs and a collection of cut crystal decanters displayed on specially fitted shelves.

Nick and Dianthe were in the forward salon. Mackenzie didn't see them at first. Dazzling light poured in from the sliding glass doors framing the room. A teak foredeck stretched outside the glass, dotted with potted palms and rattan furniture cushioned in blue and yellow stripes. The sea sparkled an achingly beautiful aquamarine just beyond the ship's prow.

With Alexander crowding her shoulder, Mackenzie stopped just inside the salon and waited for her eyes to adjust to the light. Gradually, she made out the circular conversation pit upholstered in white leather. The wall-size screen and projection unit built into one bulkhead. The tall, bronzed male in a navy blazer. The petite brunette holding a blue-steel, crosshatched pistol trained at his heart.

Well, that settled the question of whether Nick and Dianthe were in this together! With a small puff, Mackenzie let out the breath she hadn't realized she was holding.

"Ah, here you are," the countess said with genial hospitality. "Do come in, Ms. Blair, and make yourself comfortable."

Mackenzie's glance shot to Nick. Cool and unruffled and apparently unfazed by the semiautomatic aimed at his midsection, he searched her face. "Are you all right?"

"I'm fine."

"No aftereffects from the drug Dianthe informed me she injected?"

"Just a slight headache and a burning desire to kick some butt."

He smiled then, his teeth a slash of white against

his tanned skin. "Funny. I'm experiencing exactly the same feeling."

"Nicolas!" the countess protested. "The drug was necessary, you understand. Unfortunate, but necessary."

"Actually, I don't understand. Suppose you explain it to me?"

"I will, I promise you. But first, why don't you sit down? There on the sofa."

The muzzle of the gun swung left, found a bead on Mackenzie's chest, stayed steady until Nick complied.

"You, too, Ms. Blair. No, at the other end of the sofa. I wouldn't want Nick to do anything foolish, like try to throw himself in the line of fire to protect you should matters, well, get out of hand."

Icy fingers danced down Mackenzie's spine. The countess had scripted out this scene well in advance, orchestrated every move. The woman knew damned well Nick might take chances with his own life but wouldn't risk hers.

Gripping the gold money clip in a clammy fist, Mackenzie sank into the creamy leather at one end of the circular sofa. She could only pray Dianthe's every word was being beamed over NASA's new, robust microelectro-mechanical system for interplanetary communications. Swallowing the lump in her throat, she eyed the buttons in the console at the end of the couch. It never hurt to have a backup system.

The countess read her mind. "Those buttons operate the onboard intercom, but no one will hear if you should try to call for help. As I explained to the crew, Monsieur Jensen had expressed a desire to take his *chère ami* on a moonlight cruise after cocktails. A very private moonlight cruise. They were quite pleased to be given the night off."

Thus eliminating any pesky witnesses. Mackenzie had to admire the woman's thoroughness, even as she curled her fingers into claws and wished for ten seconds, just ten, free of the damned cuffs. She got her wish, but not exactly in the way she'd hoped for.

"Alexander, my sweet, get the ropes."

The younger man crossed the salon and snagged two skeins of thin, woven hemp. They were neatly looped and knotted, handy for securing launches to the dock, Mackenzie guessed. Not to mention securing potentially troublesome guests.

"Nick first," the countess instructed. "Be careful. It would be most unfortunate if he gets you in a stranglehold and I had to shoot through you to…"

"I know what to do, Dianthe." Keeping the sofa between him and Nick, the muscular youth slipped the knots and shook out a length of rope. "Arms behind you."

Nick didn't move. His face expressionless, he assessed the woman standing across the salon.

The small, ringed hand holding the pistol whitened at the knuckles. She kept the muzzle aimed squarely at Mackenzie's heart and answered his unspoken question.

"I'm afraid I have no choice, darling. It's my neck or yours. Yours and Ms. Blair's."

She'd pull the trigger. Nick didn't doubt that for a second. He'd have to buy some time, create a distraction, get Mackenzie out of the line of fire before he made his move. With casual nonchalance, he shot his cuffs to straighten the sleeves of his blazer and brought his wrists behind his back.

It was a long shot, but the jacket's sleeves might—just *might*—keep pretty boy from noticing the almost imperceptible bulge strapped to Nick's forearm.

Danton looped the rope several times, made a knot and gave it a vicious yank. Every nerve in Nick's body jumped to attention when the man's knuckles brushed cloth, but his face showed only cool contempt.

"Now Ms. Blair, my pet. We can't have her found in chains, can we?"

A dead weight formed in Nick's stomach. He didn't have to be told why Dianthe wanted to trade steel for hemp. Rope would burn and, with luck, leave no evidence that a victim had been restrained. Chain wouldn't.

So she was planning another accident. An electrical short, maybe, with a resulting fire. Or a broken fuel line, spewing gas. The fire would have to burn hot and fast to consume the *Sea Nymph* before the harbormaster saw the smoke and sent out the tugs. His mind racing, Nick worked the options while Danton exchanged Mackenzie's cuffs for rope.

Flashing him a look of utter contempt, she settled back on the sofa and turned to Nick. "Did I tell you I did some shopping this morning?"

Lord, she was cool! If Nick hadn't already fallen and fallen hard for OMEGA's brilliant, stubborn, incredibly sexy communications chief, he would have tumbled into love with her at that moment. His eyes glinting with admiration, he followed her lead.

"You mentioned you were going to hit the rue de France."

"I happened onto a very unique shop." Her glance drifted to the countess. "One that specializes in beaded evening bags."

Beaming in approval, Dianthe relaxed her tight-fisted grip on the pistol. "So you traced the purse Nick stole from me all those years ago! How very clever of you."

"It was, wasn't it? I still haven't figured out what was in the bag, though."

"Nor has anyone else, thank heavens." She paused, teasing her audience before deigning to share her knowledge. "It was one of those old-fashioned disks—floppies, I believe they were called back then. It fit perfectly inside the lining of my purse."

"A computer disk," Nick murmured.

Damn! He couldn't believe he'd missed a floppy disk. He must have been in a hurry to get the stolen purse to Gireaux. Or been so satisfied with the wallet and other trinkets inside the bag he'd let himself get careless.

"What was on this disk?" he asked with more than idle curiosity.

"I had no idea at the time, but the gentleman who left his briefcase so temptingly open while we amused ourselves was quite high-ranking and privy to all sorts of secrets. I rather hoped he'd pay a good sum to get the disk back. Through an anonymous third party, of course."

"Of course."

Nick had long suspected the countess of supplementing her income with a little discreet blackmail. Alexander had evidently suspected his mistress of the same felonious inclinations. "Who was this high-ranking gentleman?" he asked casually. "One who could afford to satisfy even your extravagant appetites, I would assume.''

''Alexander!'' With a little *tch-tch,* his mistress shook her dark curls. ''Surely you've spent enough time with me by now to know I would never bore you by going on about my past loves.''

In other words, Nick thought grimly, she had no intention of trusting Danton or anyone else with her secrets.

''How could I have known some clever little street urchin would steal my bag the very next morning?'' she continued on a note of amused chagrin. ''Do you remember that morning, Nicolas?''

''Should I?''

The blasé response implied there was nothing worth remembering about that particular day, Countess d'Ariancourt included. Dianthe didn't miss the barb. A hint of color rose in her cheeks, but the smile stayed on her lips.

''I had just walked out of the Ritz-Carlton, in Cannes, and was waiting for the valet to deliver my car. You bumped into me, apologized charmingly and sauntered off. After a night of the most delicious decadence, my wits weren't quite as sharp as they should have been. I didn't realize you'd relieved me of my purse until I went to tip the valet.''

''How inconvenient for you.''

''Yes, it was, you wretch. I spent a considerable

sum trying to track you. As did my high-ranking gentleman friend, who couldn't understand at first just how you'd obtained his disk. I fed him some tale of hearing noises during the night, I think. He became convinced a young, nimble cat burglar had slipped into our room.''

Her show of amusement faded, and chagrin gave way to real regret.

''At the time, I was more annoyed over losing my Marjorie Pelletier than a potential source of income. After a while, I put both out of my mind.''

''Who or what brought them back?''

''Your old associate, Jacques Gireaux.'' Her nose wrinkled in distaste. ''Such a rude, unpleasant individual. I can't understand why you did business with him for so long.''

''Rogues come in all sizes and personalities, Dianthe.''

No implied insult this time. It was right there, out in the open. The countess pursed her lips, but let the comment pass.

''I take it Gireaux found the disk?'' Nick asked.

''He did. He sat on it for years, though, before he sold it on the black market. Then, as you Americans are so fond of saying... You do consider yourself American now, don't you, Nicolas?''

''I do.''

"Well, as you would say, all hell broke loose. Perhaps you read about the unfortunate explosions that destroyed several Saudi oil refineries some months back?"

The tendons in the back of Nick's legs went as tight as steel cables. Carefully, he avoided looking in Mackenzie's direction.

"I've read about them."

"Evidently, the floppy disk I stole—and you in turn stole from me, you naughty boy—contained the complete engineering specifications for those refineries. As I but recently learned, the plans were drawn up by the Soviets, who hoped to capitalize on the wave of anti-American sentiment sweeping the Middle East after the Iranian embassy takeover. They not only provided the plans for the refineries, they sent a whole cadre of engineers to Saudi Arabia to help build them."

So that was the Russian involvement Ace's last message hinted at! The Russians hadn't had a hand in blowing up the refineries. They'd built the damned things.

"I think I've got the picture," Nick said with a sardonic smile. "Gireaux heard the Saudis put a million-dollar bounty on the head of the person or persons who'd provided the detailed information about the refineries' inner workings. He figured the

Saudis would eventually trace the plans back to him. And through him, to Countess d'Ariancourt.''

''*Exactement*. Gireaux intended to disappear, but first he contacted me. For some reason, he thought I'd pay him dearly not to divulge how the plans had come into his possession.''

''Instead, you had him tortured and shot.''

''It's a million-dollar bounty, Nicolas. A million dollars! Someone was sure to try to claim it. I had no choice but to destroy any and all links between me and the disk.''

If the situation weren't so damned tense, Nick would have laughed at the irony. He'd sent one of OMEGA's best agents into the field, had kept Ace sweating it out for months trying to dig up a lead as to who'd engineered those devastating explosions. He still didn't know who'd actually set the charges, but he now knew the source of their technical expertise.

''I'm told Gireaux held out for some hours,'' the countess continued with a little moue of distaste, ''but he finally revealed the name of the pickpocket who'd brought him the bag. Then, of course, I had to find the urchin. Imagine my surprise when I discovered that the thief was none other than my darling, darling Nick.''

A mingled curiosity and greed colored her voice.

"Just how much have you stolen over the years? That emerald necklace alone must have been worth a million francs."

Nick didn't bother to tell her that his thieving days had ended decades ago. Nor did he deny responsibility for the stolen emeralds. He didn't owe this woman a damned thing, much less an explanation.

"I was tempted," she continued, "sorely tempted, to use my newfound knowledge to financial advantage. Unfortunately, I couldn't take the risk with that bounty hanging over my head."

She heaved a sigh of regret, but the melodramatics didn't fool anyone. Dianthe was driven by only one consideration...saving her own skin.

"After that bungled affair in Washington, I fully expected you to turn up in Nice. I didn't, however, expect you to survive the plunge down the cliff. Now, as much as it pains me, you and Ms. Blair must experience another tragic accident. Is the launch ready, Alexander?"

"It's been ready for the past half hour. I'm merely waiting for you to finish your recital before I douse the cabin with fuel."

"Didn't I tell you?" The older woman smirked at Mackenzie. She actually *smirked!* "He's always so thoughtful. And so very, very thorough."

Dianthe's gaze followed him to the can stashed in a corner of the salon. She showed nothing but calm determination as he walked backward, splashing clear, colorless liquid from the red-painted can.

Mackenzie's nostrils flared at the acrid stench. Her throat tight, she pressed her thumb frantically against the back of the money clip. She had no idea at this point whether she'd just opened or closed a channel, but she had to keep trying.

"You'd better think what you're doing here, you overdressed, over-the-hill pervert. It's murder. In the first degree. With malice aforethought."

"Please, Ms. Blair. Let's not end matters on an exchange of insults. It's so very déclassé."

"Up yours, Countess."

With another sigh, the woman moved to the sliding glass door. "Do be careful not to splash any of that on yourself, Alexander. We shouldn't want to explain traces of gasoline on your clothing."

"Wait in the launch, Dianthe. I'll finish up here."

She cocked her head. "Will you, my pet? How generous of you. Particularly after you refused to doctor the wine I'd selected to send out to Nick's driver. I had to do it myself, once you'd left the room."

The gentle rebuke froze Alexander in his tracks.

Mackenzie had never believed in the old cliché about hair standing straight up, but every follicle on her body sent out an urgent S.O.S. Once again she sensed dark undercurrents, a dangerous tension between the countess and her lover. There was something going on between these two she didn't understand, something reflected in Alexander's face as he slowly turned to face his mistress.

Her skin crawling, Mackenzie shot a look at Nick. His shoulders were bunched and straining under the navy blazer, his expression one of grim determination as he stared at the gun in the countess's hand, now aimed at the bright red gasoline can her lover held.

"There's less than half a liter left in the can," Alexander said slowly, distinctly. "A bullet might cause it to explode, but the explosion wouldn't destroy the whole boat, Dianthe."

"Not the boat, perhaps. Just my last links to those damnable plans."

"Including me, I assume."

"Including you. *Au revoir, mon cher.*"

With a last, desperate twist of his wrist, Nick sliced through skin and hemp. Lunging across the sofa, he knocked Mackenzie to the floor at the same instant the countess fired.

His dive must have distracted her and thrown off

her aim. Either that, or she was a hell of a bad shot. The first bullet missed the gasoline can and hit Alexander, spinning him around. The second shattered the wall-size screen of the entertainment center.

Live sparks jumped from the electronic boxes behind the screen and accomplished what the first bullet had failed to do. With a loud whoosh, the gas fumes filling the cabin ignited. The flames leaped to the ceiling, arced down to the floor. Like a hissing sea serpent, they raced along the trail of spilled fuel.

Over the roar of the fire, Nick heard the glass door slam back on its runners. Dianthe was gone, rushing down to the launch no doubt, but she was the last of his concerns at the moment. Heat searing his skin, he rolled Mackenzie onto her stomach and sliced through the ropes around her wrists.

"Make for the deck," he shouted as he struggled out of his blazer and threw it over her head. "I'll bring Danton."

She didn't need a second urging. Clutching the blazer with one hand, she raced for the glass doors. Her other hand frantically worked the gold money clip.

"We're on fire! Control, do you copy? The boat's on fire."

Hooking a fist in the collar of the man lying in a

pool of blood, Nick dragged him to the door. The
flames followed them out onto the deck, hissing and
spitting and feasting on the layers of varnish that
protected the polished teak. Fire licked at Nick's
heels as he propped Danton against the rail, hooked
an arm under his knees, and heaved.

The wounded man hit with a splash. Nick and
Mackenzie dived in after him.

Chapter 14

Mackenzie surfaced to a maelstrom of noise and confusion. Fire crackled and hissed from the burning yacht. An outboard motor gunned in the distance. Another engine—larger, louder—roared toward them from the shore.

Spraying water in a high arc, Mackenzie flung her wet hair out of her face and searched the sea around her. A head topped by a tawny pelt broke the surface scant yards away. A second later, another bobbed up beside the first.

"Nick!"

With sharp scissors kicks, Mackenzie cut through the water. Her heart thumped at scorch marks on the shoulders and collar of Nick's shirt.

"Are you okay?"

"Yeah."

They had to shout to be heard over the approaching boat. No, not boat, Mackenzie saw from the corner of one eye. It was a hydrofoil, one of those passenger ferries that traveled between the Mediterranean islands, skimming inches above the water on twin pontoons.

"What about Danton?"

Not that Mackenzie particularly cared about the man floating facedown in the water. She didn't have a real soft spot in her heart for guys who splashed gasoline around with every intention of making a human shish kebab out of her.

Nor did Nick. Rolling the injured man over with less than gentle hands, he hooked an elbow around his throat to keep him afloat. Blinking the water from his eyes, he speared a hard glance over Mackenzie's shoulder. She twisted around, squinted through the glare of sunlight on the sea, and picked out the trail of spray thrown up by a white launch as it sped toward a rocky promontory.

Dammit! That had to be the countess. She'd certainly made tracks.

Her jaw tight, Mackenzie paddled one-handed and fingered the silver earring still dangling from her left lobe. She'd lost the gold money clip when she cannonballed into the sea, but the transmitter embedded in her earring might still work…assuming the folks manning the control center could have heard her over the thunderous roar of the hydrofoil, that is.

Giving up any attempt at communications for the time being, Mackenzie scowled at the launch. It was now only a tiny speck, visible for just a second or two more before it rounded the jutting finger of rock and disappeared.

''You can run,'' she muttered under her breath, ''but you can't hide. Not for long, anyway.''

Nick reclaimed her attention with a terse shout. ''Start swimming! The ship could blow at any moment.''

A quick glance at the burning boat was more than enough to get Mackenzie moving. Fed by the spilled gasoline, highly flammable deck varnish and God knew what else, the flames now consumed the *Sea Nymph's* entire upper deck. Mackenzie had no idea where the yacht's fuel tanks were located or how long it would take the fire to reach them. She wasn't about to stick around to find out.

Slicing through the green water, she aimed for the rapidly approaching hydrofoil. Nick swam with her, his strokes strong and sure, his elbow still hooked under Danton's chin. They left a thin, swirling trail of red behind them, generating a new and entirely different worry in Mackenzie's mind.

Did sharks swim in these waters?

"Lord, I hope not!"

She'd no sooner muttered that fervent wish than the water around her began to churn. Gulping, she searched the roiling surface for sail-like fins. It took a few frantic moments before she realized the waves were generated by the downwash from a chopper.

She hadn't heard the helo's approach above the roar of the hydrofoil, hadn't noticed its shadow skimming across the bay. But there it was, hovering fifty feet above the sea, close enough to whip up the water, but far enough that the waves didn't swamp her or Nick.

A uniformed crewman hung on to a handle beside the open hatch with one hand and tossed out life preservers with the other. Just behind him, Mackenzie caught a glimpse of a thin face topped by short, spiked red hair. Only then did she notice that the helo's markings identified it as belonging to Nice's Prefecture of Police.

She squirmed into one of the buoyant donuts, then helped Nick with Alexander. When she tugged one arm to force it through the preserver, the younger man groaned. He opened his eyes, stared at Mackenzie in dazed confusion. His lips moved again, but his words got lost in the deafening *whump-whump* of the helo's rotors.

At Nick's signal, the uniformed crewman keyed his mike. The chopper dropped until its skids kissed the waves. Hooking a second line to his safety harness, the rescuer took a wide-legged stance at the open hatch.

"This one!" With a combination of shouts and gestures, Nick signaled for him to take Danton first. "Careful, he's wounded."

Hand over hand, the crewman reeled Alexander in. Mackenzie went next. She got a foot on the skids, grabbed a reaching hand, and scrambled aboard.

Nick followed moments later. He flopped onto the chopper's corrugated metal deck, water dripping from his hair. The remains of his scorched shirt were plastered to his shoulders and chest. He skimmed a quick look down Mackenzie's equally bedraggled person and flashed her a rueful grin.

"That's one limo and one yacht, Blair. We're leaving quite a trail of burning hulks behind us."

"No kidding," she shouted back. "With our luck, this helo won't make it to shore in one piece."

The words were hardly out of her mouth before the *Sea Nymph* exploded. The blast produced waves of concussed air that tipped the chopper over onto its side. Its right skid went into the bay. The overhead rotors sliced water. While the passengers in the back scrabbled frantically for handholds, the pilot fought the controls.

When he finally had his craft level again, he sent it skimming toward shore. The flight engineer slammed the hatch shut, reducing the whine of the engines from a high-pitched scream to a muted roar, and grabbed a first-aid kit. The countess's lover was still bleeding from the bullet wound. His blood mixed with seawater to form rivulets of pale pink. Inspector Picard knelt next to the crewman and looked the injured man over.

Mackenzie caught her flicker of stunned amazement and remembered Alexander had been out playing tennis when the inspector and Nick interviewed the countess and her staff. This was Picard's first glimpse of Danton's muscular body, dark, curly hair and sensual mouth. Even half-drowned and swimming in his own blood, the murdering bastard could cause heart palpitations.

Regaining her composure, the inspector addressed Mackenzie. "I listened in to your transmissions, Mademoiselle Blair. Europol made the connection, through an unidentified agency in Washington."

Yes! Her people had come through.

"I'm unclear, though, how you came to be aboard the *Sea Nymph,* chained to a bed."

"The chains were compliments of Countess d'Ariancourt. And this guy."

Picard glanced at the prone man again, her expression carefully neutral this time. "He is the countess's lover, I presume. Alexander Danton?"

"You presume right."

"I promised you I would run inquiries," Picard said to Nick. "There is no Alexander Danton matching this one's description. He does not exist."

Her words penetrated the injured man's haze of pain. Grimacing, he opened his eyes. The cords in his throat worked as he ground out a few hoarse words.

"I…am…Dan*ov*. Alexander Danov. FSB."

Mackenzie's jaw dropped. The guy was an agent, working for Russia's Federal Security Bureau, successor to the old KGB?

No way!

She threw an astonished glance at Nick, who appeared more thoughtful than surprised.

"I must have missed something here?" she exclaimed. "Has the Cold War heated up again? Best I recall, U.S. and Russian agents haven't been in the business of bumping each other off since Khrushchev."

"I would not…have let you die." Danton— Danov—pulled his lips back in a grimace that was meant as a smile. "But I would have…much enjoyed…performing for Dianthe…with you."

"Pervert," Mackenzie muttered, although an answering grin tugged at her lips.

Nick didn't appear to find the exchange particularly amusing. "Good thing you *didn't* perform, Danov. If you had, you'd still be aboard the *Sea Nymph,* fried to a crisp by now."

"Of that I have no doubt."

"What's your connection to the countess?" Nick asked him. "Other than the obvious."

"My mission was to discover how…she acquired the refinery plans." The explanation obviously cost him. Gritting his teeth against the pain, he struggled to continue. "My country…is anxious…to plug the leak. Appease the Saudis. We need their oil."

"Who does not?" Picard interjected dryly. "It is no wonder Countess d'Ariancourt resorted to such extreme measures to cover her role in the destruction of these refineries."

"Speaking of the countess…" Nick slewed around to the inspector. "If you were listening in to the transmissions, you know she's escaped. Perhaps you should get on the radio and put out an all-points-bulletin."

"I have already issued the alert. My people are searching the harbor as we speak."

"She took the ship's launch and rounded the

cliffs to the west. I believe there's a fishing village just beyond the promontory. Belle Sur, isn't it?''

"*Oui.* Belle Sur.''

Reaching for the radio clipped to her waistband, the inspector issued instructions to expand the search to the west immediately.

"We shall apprehend her,'' she promised Nick when she'd finished, "and prosecute her to the full extent of the law. We have little tolerance for murderers in Nice. Or,'' she added, "for thieves.''

Uh-oh. She'd heard that part of the transmission, had she? In all the excitement, Mackenzie had forgotten all about it.

"About these stolen emeralds, monsieur...''

"Why don't we discuss them later?'' Nick suggested with a bland smile. "After we get this man to a hospital and have the countess in custody.''

"As you wish. But discuss them we shall.''

Medical attendants and a wheeled gurney were waiting when the police chopper touched down on the helo pad at Nice's L'Hôpital St. Roch. The attendants ducked under the whirling blades to retrieve their patient, then rushed him to the E.R.

Mackenzie accepted the loan of a hospital robe to cover her still drenched and rather revealing white silk slacks and top, but shook her head when

Nick suggested a doctor take a look at her rope burns.

"I'd just as soon not go into another explanation of those ropes and chains, thank you. But I would like to check on Jean-Claude while we're here. This is the same hospital he was brought to, wasn't it?"

Inspector Picard confirmed the driver was upstairs, in I.C.U. "I'll remain with Monsieur Danov. I have a number of questions for him. And for you, Monsieur Jensen, when you're prepared to answer them."

Nodding, Nick escorted Mackenzie out of the E.R. His rubber-soled deck shoes squeaked on the white tile floor. Dragging in a breath heavy with the scent of antiseptic, Mackenzie shook her head.

"I *knew* someone would recognize those damned emeralds. You'll have to give them back, Nick."

"Too late. I've already given them to you."

"Then I'll give them back. I don't have any desire to go home and try to explain to the president of the United States—not to mention Maggie and Adam—how I left OMEGA's director sitting in the *bastille.*"

"The necklace is paid for, Mackenzie."

"Huh?"

Grinning at her somewhat less than articulate response, he slid his hands under the lapels of her borrowed robe. "I made the necessary arrangements the morning after I lifted the emeralds from Gireaux's hidden safe.''

''Why?''

''They match your eyes. I want you to have them.'' He tugged on the lapels, brought her up on her toes. ''More to the point, I want you.''

His mouth brushed hers. Gently at first. Then not so gently. When he raised his head, Mackenzie's pulse hammered and her heart thumped painfully against her ribs.

''Let's go see how Jean-Claude's doing,'' she got out breathlessly. ''After that, we go back to the Negresco. As I recall, we have some unfinished business to take care of.''

A half hour later, Nick was sprawled flat on his back.

Mackenzie straddled his hips, her face flushed, her hair a damp tangle. Palms planted on his shoulders, she tightened her muscles. Slowly, she raised up on her haunches. Just as slowly, she came down.

Nick broke out in a sweat, but resisted the urge to dig his fingers into the taut curve of her butt and accelerate the action. He'd sensed her need to take the lead almost from the moment the door to their suite closed behind them. She was making up for those hours of helplessness aboard the *Sea Nymph,* he guessed, and he was more than willing to help her get them out of her system.

If he didn't die first.

He came damned close to doing just that when she raised up on her haunches again. Her breasts swung a tantalizing few inches from his mouth. Her eyes gleamed as deep and dark as a glen hidden deep in a primal forest. Slowly, so slowly, she sank down again.

His low growl curved her lips in a feline smile.

"You have a problem, Nick?"

"You know damned well I do. How long you planning to stick to this pace?"

"As long as it takes," she purred.

Which turned out to be shorter than either of them anticipated. Another slow slide, and her breath started to come in little pants. One more, and Nick satisfied a few of his own needs. His hands planed over her flanks, her bottom, the smooth line of her waist. Wrapping an arm around her middle, he brought her close enough for his tongue to touch and taste and tease.

When his teeth closed over one nipple, she gave a little gasp and bent down to give him better access. The contortion wedged her hips into his, shredding the last of Nick's restraint. He surged up, she came down and a wild, glorious free-for-all ensued.

Somewhere in the middle of it, Nick managed to rein himself in enough to thrust his hands into her hair. Breathing hard and fast, he stilled her frantic writhing.

"Mackenzie…"

"What!"

"I meant what I said in the police chopper. If Danov had hurt you, I would have left him aboard the *Sea Nymph* to fry."

"I believe you."

"Dianthe's neck is still on the chopping block."

"Okay. Good. Whatever." Squirming, she tried to pick up the rhythm again.

Nick's fists tightened in her hair. "Hold on a minute!"

"Why?"

"I'm trying to tell you I love you, dammit."

"I love you, too. Now can we get back to…"

"What did you say?"

Thoroughly exasperated, she quit wiggling. "I said I love you, too."

"Since when?"

Quivering with impatience, Mackenzie creased her forehead. Her mind was mush, her body screamed with need. She tried, she really tried, but couldn't quite organize her thoughts enough to pinpoint the exact moment she'd tumbled into love with Nick Jensen.

"Since I don't know when," she finally admitted. "Somewhere between being so pissed I zapped you with that cattle prod and ten minutes ago, I'd guess."

"That's good enough for me," Nick responded with a grin. "And speaking of prods…"

Rolling her over, he pressed her into the bed and buried himself in her wet, satiny flesh.

The afternoon had faded to dusk when a loud, protesting rumble broke the stillness.

"Is that you or me?" Nick asked lazily.

Mackenzie raised her head, turned to face him, and flopped back down on the pillow. She didn't have an ounce of strength left in her body.

"Me."

"Want to get dressed and go out to dinner? You've yet to sample Nice's haute cuisine," he reminded her.

"I don't think I could crawl out of this bed if it was on fire."

"Stay right where you are then. I'll take care of feeding you."

He meant that literally, she soon discovered. She dozed off while waiting for room service to deliver their meal and only woke when Nick wheeled a cart crammed with silver-domed plates into the bedroom.

"Voilà, madam. We have here a sample of Nice's finest dishes."

Evidently being drugged, shanghaied, almost toasted alive and made love to for four mind-blowing hours was enough to give a girl an appetite. Tucking the sheet up under her arms, Mackenzie devoured every morsel of succulent fish, savory vegetables and tangy cheese he placed between her lips. They finished with berries floating in a light, frothy cream.

"So what do you think we should do about it?" Nick asked, feeding her the last strawberry.

"About what?"

"About the fact that you love me and I love you."

She caught a drop of sweet red juice with her tongue and considered the matter.

"Well, I figured I'd get another job in Washington. Maybe with the navy. Not in uniform this time, but as a civilian. Or with the new Department of Homeland Security. I hear they're looking for folks with communications intelligence experience."

Frowning, Nick lowered the spoon. "You want to leave OMEGA?"

"No, I don't want to, but one of us has to, and we both know you're more important to the…"

"Bull."

"I beg your pardon?"

"You heard me. That's pure bull, Mackenzie."

"Okay, what's your solution?"

"I was thinking more along the lines of an engagement than a change of employment."

"Look, Nick, we talked about this. I can't sleep with you *and* continue to take orders from you. It wouldn't work. Not for me, anyway. Either we go into this relationship as equals or we don't go into it at all."

His sardonic glance took in the scattered pillows, rumpled sheets and empty dishes. "Looks to me like we're already in it, sweetheart."

She bristled, but he stilled further argument by suggesting a compromise.

"Maggie's due to deliver her baby any day now. Why don't we find out for sure when she plans to resume directorship of OMEGA before you start putting out resumes?"

"Well…"

"And in the meantime," he added with a glint in his eyes, "you'd better start thinking engagement rings. I saw one in Gireaux's safe that you might like. Four carats at least and an excellent…"

"Nick! No stolen diamonds! Please! You still have to explain the emeralds to Inspector Picard, you know."

"I will," he promised, sneaking out a hand to yank the sheet tucked under her arms. "Later."

Chapter 15

Using OMEGA's considerable resources, Mackenzie verified Alexander Danov's status as an FSB operative. Still tangle-haired and wearing only a clean, starchy white shirt borrowed from Nick, she was reviewing the data she'd gathered when the front desk called to inform Monsieur Jensen he had visitors. Nick issued instructions to send them up and dropped the antique phone back on its cradle.

"It's Inspector Picard," he advised her, "and your Russian admirer."

"You're kidding! Danov lost so much blood. I can't believe the doctors at the hospital have already released him."

"My guess is he didn't give them a whole lot of choice in the matter. He won't want to go back and report to his boss at the FSB that he failed to identify who leaked those technical drawings."

"I suppose you're right. The 'high ranking' lover Dianthe told us about could have moved up the chain over the years, be in a position to do even more serious damage if not identified and contained. Danov will want to be present when the countess goes down."

"Exactly."

"Maybe that's why Picard's here," Mackenzie said hopefully, blanking her computer screen. "Maybe her people have nabbed the countess, and the inspector wants to get all the players back together."

"Knowing Dianthe," Nick drawled, "I doubt it will be that easy."

He was right.

When Giselle Picard strode into the suite some moments later, her face was a study in frustration.

Danov followed more slowly. Deep grooves bracketed either side of his mouth, but he shrugged aside inquiries about his wound.

"I've taken worse injuries."

Mackenzie believed him. She'd just skimmed through a background brief that read like an action/

adventure script written with Sylvester Stallone or Bruce Willis in mind.

"We found the *Sea Nymph*'s launch tied up at Belle Sur's harbor," Picard announced, thrusting a hand through her reddish spikes. "Unfortunately, we have not found the countess."

"Great," Mackenzie muttered under her breath.

She'd had her fill of being staked out and shot at and now just wanted this operation over. In her considered opinion, Countess d'Ariancourt was becoming a major pain in the bohunkus.

Evidently Nick shared her opinion. He masked his feelings behind his usual calm, but she knew him well enough now to pick up the annoyance buried in his cool questions about roadblocks and airport alerts.

"We're searching all automobiles leaving the area," Picard said in answer to his queries, "and have put officers at the train station, the ferry dock and the airport. Monsieur Danov, however, thinks the countess remains right here, in Nice."

All eyes turned to the Russian. Leaning his good side against the back of a chair for support, he talked through his rationale.

"Dianthe is no fool. She doesn't know I'm FSB, but she certainly suspected my motives enough to put a bullet into me." His dark eyes locked with

Nick's. "I think she must also wonder who you and Mademoiselle Blair work for, Jensen."

"We work for the president of the United States. Ms. Blair provides my communications support. My title, as I suspect you're well aware, is special envoy."

"Is that your only title?"

Nick didn't so much as blink. He wasn't about to confirm OMEGA's existence to an FSB operative.

"The only one," he answered blandly.

Danov clearly had his doubts. So did Picard. She glanced from one man to the other, making no effort to disguise her impatience.

"*Whoever* you all work for, please understand that the Nice Prefecture of Police has not relinquished jurisdiction in this case."

She shot Alexander a fulminating look. He returned it with something less than his usual cynicism.

Mackenzie glanced from one to the other. She could almost feel the heat leaping between them.

Good Lord! They hadn't wasted any time. Not that she could blame Giselle Picard. The man was walking, talking sex.

"If Monsieur Danov would be good enough to tell us where he thinks his mistress may be hiding at the moment,'' the inspector snapped, ''perhaps we may wrap matters up.''

''Former mistress,'' Alexander corrected. ''The position is presently unoccupied.''

Not for long, if those smoldering looks meant what Mackenzie thought they did.

''So where is she?'' Nick asked, losing a little of his own patience. ''It's time to end this farce.''

''She rents a flat in Old Town, for when she wishes to get away from the staff and enjoy more, shall we say, private liaisons. I discovered the lease when I was going through her papers.''

''Lovely work, this spy business.''

He ignored Mackenzie's muttered aside. ''The flat is on the rue des Jardins. Perhaps you know it, Jensen?''

''No, but I'm familiar with the street. There's a phone kiosk at about the eighteen-hundred block. Europol's had it under surveillance for some days now.''

''Ah.'' Nodding, Danov fitted together his own pieces of the puzzle. ''The attack she talked about? The one in Washington? It was arranged from this kiosk?''

''That's our guess.''

''She's clever, our Dianthe. If nothing else, she's very, very clever.''

She was also shark-bait once Mackenzie got hold

of her. Almost as impatient now as Giselle Picard, she grabbed her purse.

"I have a score to settle with your Dianthe. How about we get this show on the road?"

When the SWAT team Picard hastily assembled kicked in the door of the apartment on the rue des Jardins, it wasn't the countess they found waiting inside. It was her lawyer.

The little toad sat in a stiff-backed chair. His ankles were crossed, his hands clutched a leather briefcase, and he wore a pained expression, as though he'd forgotten to drink his prune juice this morning. He said little beyond identifying himself until the apartment had been searched and a thoroughly disappointed Picard dismissed the SWAT team.

"Countess d'Ariancourt has authorized me to act as her agent in negotiations regarding any charges levied against her."

"There's nothing to negotiate," Picard said flatly.

"But there are charges?"

The inspector ticked them off on her fingers. "Conspiracy to commit murder. Kidnapping. Felonious assault with a deadly weapon. Other charges may follow. Until they do, and until we know the full extent of her crimes, we make no deals."

"Perhaps you should allow your supervisor to decide that," the attorney said. "Or one of these gentlemen."

His gaze shifted to the two men. The countess's young lover he dismissed with a sniff, but Nick held his attention.

"I am informed you wield considerable influence with your president, Monsieur Jensen. So much you might convince him to request clemency on behalf of my client."

"Why the hell should I do that?"

"The countess indicates you're quite anxious to learn the identity of the person or persons who sabotaged the Saudi oil refineries. In her quest to protect herself, she uncovered some interesting information in that regard."

"Let me get this straight. Are you saying Dianthe wants to trade information about the sabotage for her own neck?"

"Not just her neck. There's also the matter of the million-dollar bounty. She'd like it deposited to a Swiss account. I'm authorized to accept the funds for her and make the necessary transfer."

Mackenzie gave a snort of disbelief. "You can't really think we'd go along with this ridiculous scheme."

"But I do, mademoiselle, as does my client. She is perfectly sincere in the offer, I assure you. In fact, she recognizes you suffered some duress at her hands and wishes to share a portion of the bounty with you. I believe one percent was the amount she mentioned."

In eight succinct words, Mackenzie told the attorney what the countess could do with her one percent.

Highly offended, he rose and addressed Nick. "You have two hours, Monsieur Jensen. After that, my client will sever communication with me and, of necessity, disappear forever."

Nick returned to the Negresco to transmit the countess's outrageous offer to the president. Giselle Picard detoured to the precinct to report to her superiors. Alexander melted into the night, presumably to do the same.

The president and his advisors mulled the offer over for all of a half hour. Mackenzie had already figured out what the answer would be.

"Let me guess," she said when Nick terminated the secure satellite connection. "Keeping the pipelines open is more important than nailing the woman who tried to make toast of us, not once, but twice."

"You got it."

"Damn!" Thoroughly frustrated, she folded her arms around her middle and turned to gaze at the inky black bay. "I hate to see the witch get away with this!"

Nick strolled over to join her. Wrapping his arms over hers, he drew her against him. His breath stirred her hair. His long, hard length stirred a whole lot more than her hair.

"Who said she's going to get away with anything? How do you feel about a honeymoon in the Swiss Alps?"

Wiggling around, she searched his face and discovered he was serious. "A couple of hours ago, we were talking about engagement rings and waiting until Maggie has her baby and comes back to work."

"That was a couple of hours ago."

"So what's changed?"

"The fact that we're not going back to Washington just yet, and when we do, the issue of whether or not Maggie returns to work might be moot."

"Huh?"

"Never mind. Just answer the question."

"What question?"

His arms tightened, molding her to his thighs and chest. "How do you feel about honeymooning in the Swiss Alps?"

For a heartbeat or two, Mackenzie experienced

exactly the same sensation she had in those awful seconds before the limo came out of its inverted hang and careened down the cliff.

Then the wild panic evaporated and she knew, she absolutely knew, she had no reason to fight the emotions tearing through her. She loved this man. Had trusted him with her life. She'd be ten kinds of an idiot not to trust him with her heart.

Sliding her palms up his shirtfront, she hooked them around his neck. "A honeymoon anywhere sounds pretty good to me."

Chapter 16

A cold breeze rustled the leaves that had floated down from the chestnut trees lining the quiet side street just off Massachusetts Avenue. Mackenzie snuggled her chin down into the collar of her coat and pulled into a reserved parking space in front of the town house set midway down the block. September had given way to an unseasonably cold October during the weeks she and Nick had been in Europe. Unfortunately, those same weeks hadn't seen Maggie's pregnancy give way to a birth.

"I can't believe it," her former boss grumbled, grabbing Mackenzie's hand and using it to lever out of the passenger seat. "Two and a half weeks late.

If I blimp up anymore, they're going to strap TV cameras on me and float me over the RFK Stadium to cover the Monday night game.''

"That's a sight I'd pay to see.''

Tucking her arm in Maggie's, she half supported, half hauled her up the short flight of stairs.

"You laugh,'' her mentor grumbled as she waddled through the front door, "but wait until you and Nick decide to start a family. Incidentally, when *are* you and Nick going to start a family?''

"Hey, we're still on our honeymoon.''

"Some honeymoon! Only you and Lightning would stroll into a Swiss bank, somehow manage to gain access to confidential customer account records and use them to track down the bitch who hired two gunmen to shoot up my kitchen. I sincerely hope she went down hard.''

"*Very* hard.''

The image of the countess's startled face when another SWAT team had kicked in the door, this time to her hired digs in Prague, was something Mackenzie would cherish for a long, long time… almost as long as she would cherish her last sight of the slim, not-so-elegant Dianthe in an orange prison jumpsuit. Grinning at the memory, she escorted her friend and mentor into the reception area.

"Hi, Elizabeth. What's so important Nick had to interrupt my lunch with Maggie?"

"You'd better let him tell you."

Her grandmotherly face scrunching in concern, Elizabeth Wells rounded the corner of her desk to take their coats. Maggie's barely covered her bulging stomach.

"You look so uncomfortable, dear. Is there anything I can get you?"

"A *puli-puli* root would be nice. I read that the women of the Andari tribe in the Malay jungle chew them to bring on contractions."

"I'll see if I have any *puli-puli* in the pantry. If not, how about some tea?"

"Tea sounds wonderful."

"Go on in and I'll bring it to you. Nick's waiting for you."

Not just Nick, the two women discovered. Adam was there, as well, summoned from a meeting of the International Monetary Fund. He looked suavely handsome in a charcoal-gray suit, white shirt and red tie, and smiled with loving chagrin as he bent to kiss his wife.

"When Nick called me out of my meeting, I was sure it was to tell me you and Mackenzie were on your way to the hospital."

"I wish!"

Grinning at Maggie's rueful response, Mackenzie

crossed the room and slipped her hand into her husband's.

The four-karat rock Nick had purchased—legally, he swore!—glinted on her hand. She hadn't yet grown used to its weight, or to the fact she was actually married to this incredible, scintillating, sexy man. If the rest of their marriage proved as exciting as their honeymoon, the years ahead should prove interesting. Very interesting indeed!

Still, Mackenzie felt a tug of regret that the honeymoon was almost over. Nick had returned to work yesterday. She'd delayed her return another few days to finish moving her things into his Maclean town house and give Maggie moral support during her last days of misery.

The sad truth was, Mackenzie didn't look forward to officially returning, only to tell her people that she was leaving OMEGA. As Maggie had confirmed over lunch, she'd decided not to resume the directorship. Neither she nor Adam wanted to spend the long hours away from their young, growing family required of the head of OMEGA. So the job was Nick's for as long as he wanted it.

Which meant Mackenzie had to go. Her inbred sense of professionalism wouldn't let her stay. Not with her husband in charge. Aside from the fact that she couldn't see herself taking orders from the man who shared her bed, their special relationship both on and off the job wouldn't be fair to the others.

She'd miss OMEGA, though. The excitement. The around-the-clock activity. The thrill of getting first crack at every electronic innovation developed by the government.

Oh, well, this was Washington D.C. The center of the universe, at least in the view of those who lived or worked inside the beltway. She wouldn't have any trouble finding another position. With that thought firmly in mind, she smiled up at her husband.

"So why did you call Adam out of his meeting and Maggie and me away from lunch?"

"I thought it would be appropriate for OMEGA's former directors to hear the news first."

"What news?" Adam asked, his blue eyes curious. "What's going on, Nick?"

"A major governmental reorganization, with direct implications for OMEGA."

Tucking his wife's hand in the crook of his arm, Nick dug a small remote out of his pocket. One click, and the mahogany panels behind his desk slid open. Another click brought up an organizational wiring diagram. The maze of lines and boxes filled the entire screen.

"I met with the president this morning and got the green light on my proposal," Nick informed the

other three. "In the interest of closer cooperation
with the CIA and FBI, OMEGA will fold some of
its functions into a new directorate."

Thoroughly intrigued, Adam studied the complex
organizational structure. "I see you've moved Intelligence into this new directorate. And Communications."

"What?"

Mackenzie leaned forward, frowning at the chart.
Like every chief, she was highly territorial when it
came to her operation. Any uncoordinated change
would have roused her defenses. A major realignment like this had her instinctively bristling. Before
she could ask just why the heck Nick had proposed
such a sweeping change, Adam nodded approv-
ingly.

"Smart move," he commented. "Comm pro-
vides the basic infrastructure for all our operations.
By aligning it loosely within the Homeland Defense
structure, you'll increase both the immediacy of our
access and the cooperation between the various
governmental agencies."

"That was my thinking," Nick agreed. "The
head of the new directorate will remain here on the
premises, but report to the president through the
Secretary of Homeland Defense. Think you can
handle both the convoluted chain of command and
the added responsibilities, Comm?"

Still trying to take in the details of the new organization, Mackenzie blinked. "Me?"

"You."

"Of course I can. But... Well..."

She couldn't get past the awful suspicion that Nick had realigned his entire organization just to accommodate her. Surely he didn't think she'd accept a position that had been jury-rigged for her by her husband?

He read the doubt and burgeoning distaste in her face. Smiling, he spiked her guns before she could fire a broadside and scuttle the plan.

"This change has been in the works since 9-11. I couldn't tell you, as the president wanted to mull over the various options, but your name was penciled in from the start as the head of the new directorate. It means a promotion, by the way." His blue eyes gleamed. "And considerable independence in your operations."

He knew darn well that would reel her in.

"It does, huh? In that case, it sounds like a heck of a plan to me."

Grinning at her easy capitulation, he turned to Maggie. From the looks of it, OMEGA's former director entertained more than a few reservations about the realignment. Her brown eyes were narrowed, and she wore a tight, intent expression.

"You haven't said much," Nick commented. "What do you think, Chameleon?"

"What I *think*," she said slowly, "is that my water just broke."

Adam spun around. His spine went rigid when he took in the puddle pooled around his wife's feet. Pressing her hands to the sides of her belly, she gave him a lopsided grin.

"I also think...we're not going to...make it to the hospital."

Mackenzie gulped. Nick swore. Adam strode forward and swept his wife into his arms. Depositing her on the leather sofa set by the bay windows, he barked a quick order.

"Call 9-1-1, Nick. Now!"

"No...time. I'm...crowning."

Adam's jaw went tight, but he shucked his suit coat with deliberate calm and rolled up his sleeves. His eyes glinted as he positioned himself at the end of the sofa.

"As always, my darling, you do things in your own, inimitable style."

"I...try."

"Nick, get some towels, would you?"

While he headed for the washroom hidden behind another mahogany panel, Mackenzie raced to the door.

"Elizabeth! We need you!"

Whirling, she darted back to Nick's desk and hit the switch on his computer. Within seconds, she'd pulled up a raft of information on home deliveries.

Exactly fourteen minutes later, a sweat-drenched, beaming Maggie held her son in her arms. Adam had hitched a hip on the arm of the sofa. His naked vulnerability as he stroked his wife's hair put a lump in Mackenzie's throat.

Wailing sirens announced the arrival of the fire department and EMT vehicles. Mrs. Wells ushered the crews past the crowd of operatives and technicians who'd rushed downstairs when they'd heard Maggie was in labor.

The emergency medical crews surrounded mother and baby. Edging to a far corner of the office to give them room to work, Mackenzie snuggled against Nick's side and linked her hand in his.

"With Adam and Maggie for parents and us for godparents," she murmured, "what do you think the odds are that the little squirt will one day occupy this office?"

"I'd say they were pretty good. Unless Jilly or Samantha decide to go for it first."

"Now there's a thought!"

"Of course, we should consider another possibility."

"Which is?"

"You and I might have a shot at producing OMEGA's next generation. We'd have to practice a little more first. You know, make sure we've got the fundamentals down."

"Hey, I'm all for getting the fundamentals down. When's our practice session?"

Grinning, he curled a knuckle under her chin and tipped her face to his. "As soon as the office clears out. Did I ever tell you how many nights I've laid awake, plotting ways to get you naked and on the conference table?"

Mackenzie's breath caught. Any other time, she would have cringed at the thought of making love to the man who was still nominally her boss. In his office. During duty hours, no less!

But Maggie had just given birth. Adam was displaying an emotion that made her ache inside. And Nick was smiling down at her.

Mackenzie shivered with eager anticipation.

*   *   *   *   *

If you enjoyed what you just read,
then we've got an offer you can't resist!

Take 2 bestselling love stories FREE!

Plus get a FREE surprise gift!

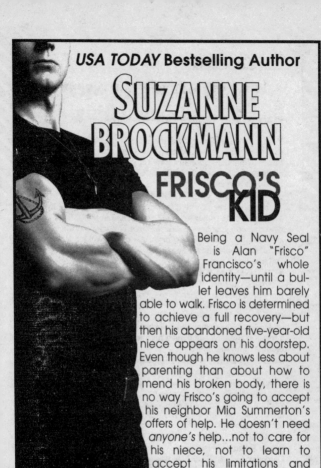

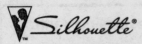